THE HURRICANE STEW

Martine Wolfe-Miller

ISBN: 0998262803
ISBN 13: 9780998262802
Library of Congress Control Number: 2016917537
Red Wolfe Publishing, Mount Pleasant, SC

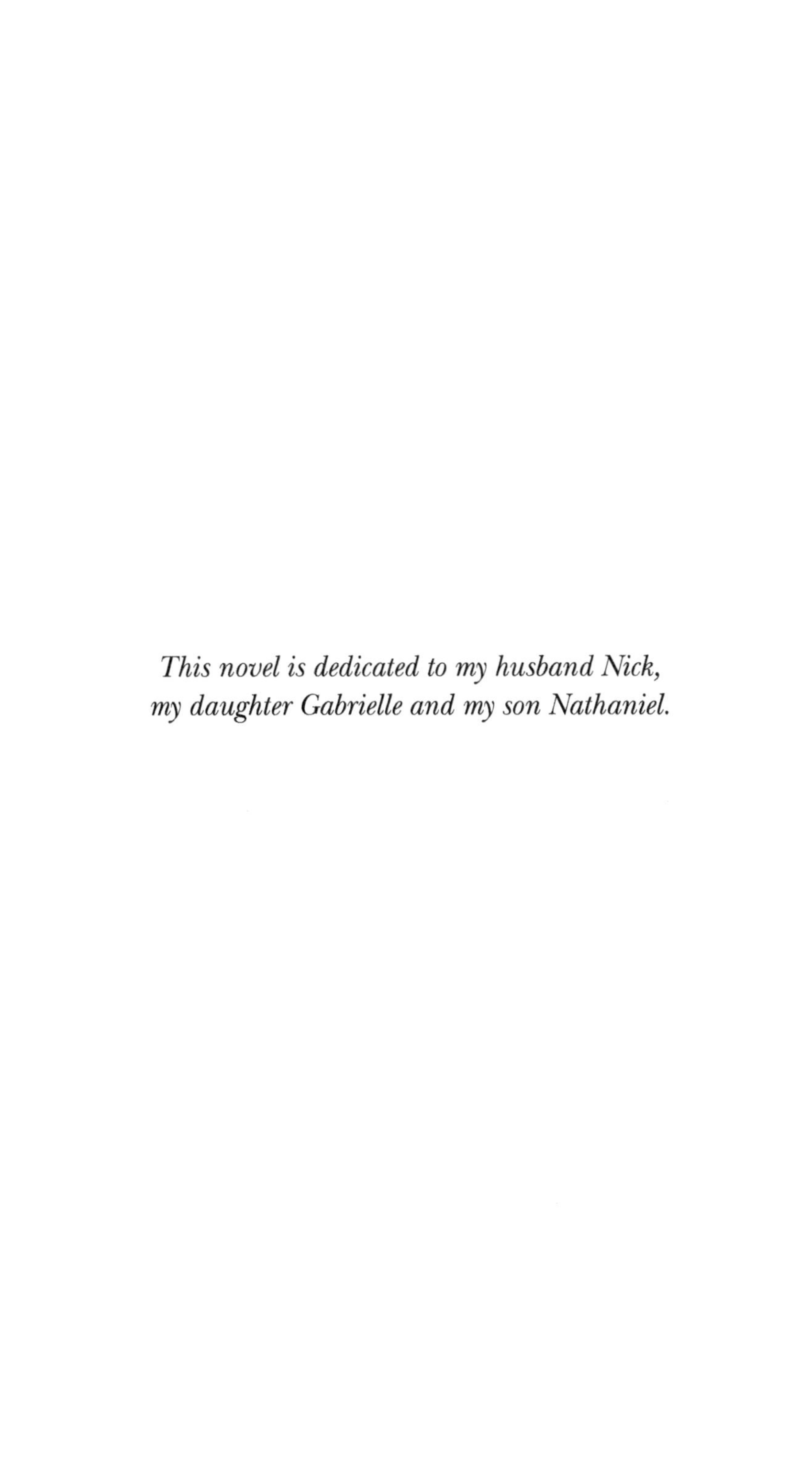

This novel is dedicated to my husband Nick,
my daughter Gabrielle and my son Nathaniel.

CHAPTER 1
TUNERS & WRITERS

On a sweltering Carolina road, David Lyle rolled his window down to keep the air moving in his aging red car. It was too hot for a dog to hunt, his friend often said. The temperamental air conditioning unit stopped working last summer and had since made his life miserable. Relief was on the way, he smiled. His piano tuning business was thriving and he planned to replace the faulty device next week. He often cursed the humidity and the shrouding heat of Carolina summers, but they were the price he paid for the crisp relief of spring, fall and winter. His Indiana blood had not thinned in the South; it was too thick for such weather.

David eased his car into an empty parking lot next to a white wooden sign. The words *Serenity, Sensitivity and Spirituality* painted in glossy black absorbed the blazing sun. An inferior concrete replica of the Bonaventure statue adorned the driveway. The pouty chubby-cheeked girl held a plastic magnolia flower in her outstretched hands. The afternoon sun singed wide swaths of centipede grass into yellow patches across the lawn.

David stepped out of his car and walked on the crushed oyster path leading to the main door. The sweat, settled between his shoulder blades, soaked the back of his shirt. Self-conscious and eager to reach colder climes, he hurried to the entrance of the funeral home.

A colorful man, decked in a pressed suit, lavender shirt with matching tie and kerchief, came out and greeted David. He ushered him into a lobby where three generations of proud Stanley Funeral Home proprietors stared at him from golden frames. Decorated in royal shades of purple, the interior of the parlor failed to convey the pomp and circumstances it aimed for. Gilded chandeliers missed a few light bulbs. The carpet showed bare thread in high traffic areas, and the blinds coughed plumes of dust in the path of an ancient pedestal fan.

Judson Stanley was a man of few words who saw no need to entertain the help. He led David to a room lined with chairs and plastic trees and left him there. In the back of the room, David recognized the upright Young Chang piano the owner had mentioned on the phone. As with the rest of the place, the piano showed signs of age and neglect.

A portable air conditioning unit moved tepid air in the clammy room. The contraption, laboring to cool the space, made annoying clinking sounds. Classical music, piped in through speakers, could not dissipate the sense of gloom that greeted David. A mélange of age, disinfectant, beeswax, mildew and gardenia stirred melancholic echoes.

Alone in the room, David opened his tuning case and set to work, removing mice droppings and broken strings, bringing an old friend back to life. Each piano told a story he enjoyed discovering. He adjusted the portable light to his forehead and worked on the keys, shaking his uneasiness. He was in a funeral home and ghosts were part of the place.

At five o'clock, Judson closed shop and retreated to his office. David heard him pour himself a drink and fumble with the radio. The classical music soon gave way to *Ain't No Mountain High Enough* and other Motown's greatest hits. David shook his head in dismay. The blaring songs made a painful tuning even worse. The darkness hampering his work, he stood up looking for an outlet and flipped the switch. Brash fluorescent light chased shadows and bounced off the silver metal polish of a casket near the far wall. Impossible to ignore, the dreary object shone in the garish room like a lighthouse calling lost souls.

David approached it with caution. The mellow voices of the Temptations coming through the speakers warned him *Don't Look Back*. However, the insistent and repetitive beat intensified his soulful quest. A few inches from the open coffin, he looked down mesmerized by the sight.

Nestled in pleats of white satin, the corpse of a shriveled black woman laid in rest. She wore an ill-fitted grey dress several sizes too large for her small frame. The touch of pink color on her cheeks belied her present circumstances. The silver curls of her new wig completed a feeble attempt at coquetry. A mortuary attendant had prepared the tiny woman for a viewing that never happened. The empty room, dark and humid, barren of flowers and people, spoke of disregard and loss.

David turned off the light, closed the door, and returned to the piano bench, his craving for silence answered. No chatty customers, rambunctious children, or curious pets he often complained about. He applied himself to the task, respectful of the departed. He worked on the upright for two hours, tuning each string with care. His work completed, he began playing Chopin's Nocturne in D flat. His fingers danced on the keys for longer than was customary. It felt odd to leave the room without bearing witness to her life.

The old woman's narrative had ended but David had just begun his story. Leaving his sales job and turning to self-employment had proven a gutsy but profitable move. He was still in awe of changes that had transformed his world into a lucrative business venture. He had landed a five-year contract with the

Watson School of Arts and owed it all to Miss Bunnie, one of his first customers. She helped him negotiate his contract and he had since tuned her piano for free. His tuning instruments packed, David left his business card with contact information inside the piano and drove to Bunnie's house.

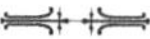

In an older part of town, a slim woman set down pen and paper with a frown. "I don't have another book in me. I painted myself in a corner and I don't know where to take the story." Bunnie Dupree sat at her desk, exasperation and disgust etched on her face.

"You took the plot to dark places," her friend answered. "Pick a name for the villain and stay with it. The reader may have trouble following your plot if you keep changing his name," she added with a smile.

Sophie Kegan, a graduate student at Watson, looked at Bunnie with affection. The art department secretary had become a friend. She relished their time together and their vigorous debates.

Bunnie had celebrated her sixty-ninth birthday last year and Sophie attended the celebration. She remembered driving to the house and knowing without looking at her GPS that she had found the place. A wisteria bush loomed over the mailbox resembling an enormous purple mushroom. The vine had grown over the decades into a large canopy, engulfing the mailbox and shading half of the road. Each year, the plant hosted nests of bees and wasps, preventing anyone from approaching the mailbox. Several painful stings had led to an uneasy truce between the U.S. Postal Service and Bunnie. The postmaster ignored her mailbox, and she picked up her mail at her neighbor's home. The purple mushroom continued to flourish, catching the occasional car antenna passing by and releasing a cloud of angry bees.

Sophie and Bunnie's friendship was instantaneous. They shared an eccentric outlook on life. Sophie attributed hers to youth and admired Bunnie for holding to her originality for so long. After seven decades, her friend had become a writer. She had penned and self-published her first book, which Sophie had read in shock. It contained a vampire's plan to terra form Mars, an arcane society and the recipe for eternal youth. The novel was a glorious mess reshaping tired clichés into impossible new plots.

Sophie was hopeful when Bunnie chose the mystery genre for her second novel. But her hope soon turned to bewilderment when her friend crafted her first murder mystery novel. In the space of three chapters, Bunnie had taken on a serial killer, a crooked cop, three murders and the nefarious world of the mafia underground.

"You may have gone too dark, too fast. Readers enjoy figuring out the 'whodunit' on their own," Sophie hinted, setting down the draft on the kitchen table.

"Less is more," she cautioned. "This is your third victim in three chapters."

"I'm fixing to make dinner now," Bunnie mumbled. "At least, I can still cook." Setting aside her murderous writing, she assembled the ingredients for her famous stuffed green peppers recipe.

The years had been kind to Bunnie. Her svelte figure belied her near septuagenarian status. Her short-cropped white hair, far from aging her, emphasized her youthful looks. She dressed and accessorized with impeccable taste and her southern drawl delighted Sophie, a northern girl at heart.

The young woman rented a room in Bunnie's house last year and had not regretted her decision. Cohabitation with Bunnie was as fun as it was unpredictable. Sophie relished solving the puzzle that was her roommate. Her opinions were so foreign to hers. Her friend's mind resembled a large antebellum mansion where rooms and additions led to strange places.

"I should not have researched my novel on my personal computer," Bunnie mused, a green pepper in hand. "I read that law enforcement monitors these sites."

Sophie stopped chopping herbs in midair and looked at her with alarm. "Which sites? Where have you been?"

"Money laundering, drug trafficking, and racketeering sites. Other places, I'd rather not mention," Bunnie blushed. "I also brushed up on autopsies and crime scenes. I can even make a bomb. Once you get on those sites, it becomes impossible to limit yourself to a single line of inquiry. They are wicked fun!"

"A bomb?" interrupted Sophie. "Why do you need a bomb in your story? Isn't Duncan Oliver an industrialist? Where could he have learned to counterfeit money, launder it and make a bomb?"

"Remember, less is more." Sophie cautioned. "Stay on task and focus on the main plot. The fetishist serial killer was already unconventional, but now a bomb?"

"Great stories are steeped in common experiences. Pick a real-life bogeyman. There must be one at school who could give you enough material to build your imaginary villain?" she suggested with a smile.

Bunnie looked at the kitchen ceiling, her gaze lingering on a spider web, and came up with an answer. "Charles Holzer! He could fit the bill. He is the school villain everybody loves to hate. Everyone is afraid of him. I have been uneasy around him myself for years. He'd make a great scoundrel!"

"Make sure you change the names to protect the innocent," replied Sophie with a nervous laugh.

She had met Charles Holzer upon first arriving to Watson. She heard him in the auditorium during convocation, along with several hundreds of her classmates. The president of the prestigious school was tall and fit with an air of command. Salt and pepper hair and deep blue eyes accented his indisputable good looks.

Patrician features brought distinction and elegance to his demeanor. His youthful smile was arresting, even if it did not reach his eyes. He was a masterful orator whose speech inspired and motivated. Yet, Sophie felt a gap between his words and the feelings he sought to elicit from the audience. Staff, while attentive and respectful, appeared subdued and uncomfortable. Sophie did not sense the camaraderie that unites teachers at the start of a school year. She had sensed fear.

CHAPTER 2
PINK SLIPS

Dr. John Wilson knocked on the Office of the President's door, prepared to discuss the renewal of his tenure as Dean of the Fine Arts Department. A voice greeted him. He let himself in and faced a sight so incongruous that he plopped, rather than sat, on the guest chair. President Holzer sat at his desk flanked to his right by Watson's Chief of Police.

John looked at his watch, uncomprehending. "Have I made a mistake about our appointment, Charles?"

He had known him for twenty years and was on a first name basis. "I thought we were meeting to discuss my tenure," he asked, glancing at the chief.

The president's face was emotionless. His voice dropped to a sliver of steel. "Yes, we are."

John sensed the barometric pressure of the room drop to a glacial depth. His back straightened in the chair. He trembled as shivers of ice traveled down his spine.

Forgoing niceties, Charles continued. "Our enrollment numbers have dropped over the past five years. This is a concern. The Board wants a fresh approach to keep students engaged. We are taking a new direction with your department."

John dared hope. The dip did not affect his department. *He's talking about the Business School,* he thought. He had been the first on staff to raise the alarm. Online universities were damaging the traditional brick-and-mortar companies. The business model for higher education was fast changing. Soaring tuition prices and the Great Recession had brought a dose of reality to academia. *About time,* John thought.

He recognized the need for an online program and snickered at Charles' hypocrisy. It was like him to blame his subordinates and not take responsibility. John could play the game, but the presence of the chief unnerved him. *What is he doing here?*

Charles crushed his hopes with a stunning remark.

"The Board has decided not to renew your tenure. They will offer you a generous severance package once you resign. This proposal is not negotiable and their decision is final. I am sorry, John, but you must decide before you leave my office."

The words unleashed their poison in the air, wisps of fear attacking his sense of identity and place in the world. The chief stood tall and firm, ready for a desperate response–an aggressive gesture. None came.

John sat in his chair unable to move. He had fallen into the rabbit hole. Reality no longer held sway. *I am being fired?*

He understood the words but could not grasp the breath of such sentence. Shame flushed his face, despite his best effort to stay calm.

A fight-or-flight response seized him. He braced himself for battle.

"I can fix this. I can integrate new technology in the curriculum. I never got the authorization to carry out the program before, but my department will offer online classes by next semester," he said with more conviction than he felt.

He knew that Charles maintained a complete hold on the Board. They would not get rid of him without his tacit approval. He sensed that the decision, wherever it came from, was final.

"Charles," John pleaded, stunned, "why?" The situation proved so surreal it choked him. Then it became clear. *I am given a way out. He knows.* The battle was over, John recognized. There was no fighting, just fleeing.

"I need your answer now."

John sank in his chair, catatonic and despondent. He gasped and uttered a muffled sound Charles heard and took as complete surrender.

"Chief, go with Dr. Wilson to Human Resources to execute his severance package. Take him to his office and help him pack his belongings," he ordered.

Charles saw a shell of a man leave his office with relief. Disposing of John was easy, given what he knew. He prided himself on keeping his staff on a tight leash. Over the past two decades, he had perfected the art of hooking them. He enjoyed watching his colleagues succumb to their dark sides. Addiction, for most, turned to sex, alcohol and drugs. It was so predictable.

Following their hiring, Charles inducted his upper management staff in a world of tempting rewards and benefits. Staff attended lavish business trips and all expenses paid conferences. He kept them pliable and dependent on the school for their summer frolics. The per diem was generous and not documented by the administration. He enjoyed watching their slow dance into thievery. Few resisted the temptation and most fell. After several indiscretions, employees found themselves outside the law, looking in with dread. Charles' true gift was to keep them in this nebulous state, never knowing if someone was on their trail. Thieves often start small, but a wandering hand in a cookie jar seldom stops at one.

The chief proved useful, but he had not escaped the snare. He often operated outside of legal boundaries to complete his assignments. Charles recorded each infraction with meticulous zeal. He believed in precise documentation and kept a file on everyone.

People were seldom original in their pursuits, but Dr. Wilson had surprised him. John stumbled after a decade of perfect service and untainted record. His obsession with rare stamps brought him into Charles' line of sight. It was an odd passion to gamble reputation, career and integrity.

The president began monitoring John's trips to Europe with renewed interest. His undocumented acquisitions grew into a large collection of stolen rare stamps. Charles did not interfere and watched. John's indiscretions began five summers ago. Was it boredom setting in after the death of Margaret, his wife of thirty years? His moral compass gone, was it easier for John to live a life unexamined?

While updating his personal files on several of his staff, Charles noticed a discrepancy. He compared a bill of sale from Villa Vittoria, near Florence, with Watson's ledger. The mystery proved easy to unravel. He contacted his suppliers overseas and soon learned about the stamps. John's school acquisitions were impressive and had improved Watson's standing in the art community. Thieves often rationalize their wandering hands, Charles suspected. John may have thought that his stamps were a justifiable finder's fee for his hard work.

Over the past few years, the president noticed that John's discretionary spending had decreased, and that some stolen stamps were now part of the official school's inventory. It concerned him. Was John preparing to wean himself of his dependency? Was he giving his loot back? It appeared that way. John was at heart good and principled, eager to get back on the right side of justice. Charles recognized that his window of opportunity and his advantage were fast closing. His prey was returning to his boring law-abiding self. He had to act to protect what was at stake. John had to go.

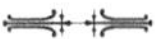

Nine hundred miles north on the east coast, Dr. Marie Caldwell and her young daughter Isabelle sat in the cab of a rental moving truck. A perky potted plant stood between them, a promise of new beginnings. Marie looked at the sky in disbelief as clouds appeared, soon followed by gusts of wind and the arrival of rain. She felt the winds of fortune turn. Doubts clouded her minds and immobilized her.

The office manager rushed outside. "You'll be OK? I can drive the truck out of the lot for you. The gate is narrow."

"No. I better get the hang of it now," Marie thanked him, eager to get going. The large truck was automatic and should be easier to drive than a stick shift. She drove a tractor once and remembered to give a large berth to objects and people. She was towing her car and needed to accommodate the added torque.

Marie took a deep breath and looked at the smiling face of her daughter. Isabelle had taken to their cross-country trip like a pirate to a treasure hunt. This comforted Marie and calmed her nerves. She inserted the key in the ignition and started the engine. Easing the truck through the parking lot, she bade goodbye to her life in the Northeast. She planned to reach the Carolinas in less than two days and she could not stop her momentum now. She glanced in the mirror as she passed the gate. Her last memory was of the rental manager's face frozen in fear as she narrowly missed the left post of the gate. A few minutes later, she was speeding on the highway.

Her vehicle tested her resolve within miles of leaving the rental yard. Eighteen-wheelers barreling down I-81 shook her truck and shattered her confidence. She lost her air conditioning within two hours and her poise in the same breath. Wiping tears from her cheeks, she kept on driving. Isabelle had fallen asleep unaware of her mother's distress. *This is a mistake,* she thought between silent sobs. The new job at Watson University was a mistake. Leaving her tenured position at the University of Scranton was a mistake. She had not yet taken ownership of her new life that she was having buyer's remorse. She faced a past life she could not hold onto and a new one she was afraid to claim.

Marie stayed on course for five hours despite her mounting anxiety. She was looking for a rest stop when she observed a weight station flashing trucks to enter. Obeying the highway sign, she followed colossal eighteen-wheelers and waited in line for her turn to weigh in. An exasperated highway worker gestured her to move past the scale.

"Move along! What do you think you are doing? You are not a truck! Move!" he yelled.

Marie felt rejected and that emotion soon bled onto her entire life. She grabbed the stirring wheel, stretched her limbs and settled herself in the driver's seat. They had four more hours until midway and a welcome night at the hotel. Determined to regain control of herself, she sped along and got back on the highway. Massive steel creatures passed her by, spewing exhaust in their wake.

CHAPTER 3

LOWCOUNTRY BOIL

"What happened to Dr. Wilson?" asked Sophie, peeling potatoes and wondering about the latest school drama.

"Nobody knows, least of all Dr. Wilson," Bunnie answered. "With that award he won, and several of the grants he got last year, I thought his job was secure."

"Money?" Sophie countered.

"President Holzer is tighter than bark on tree," Bunnie said. "But I don't think money was the reason. He just hired Dr. Caldwell to help with the department. I wonder what she's making of her new boss, gone a week before her start date. We'll find out soon enough. I have invited her to dinner tonight."

"Why not appeal? There must be a grievance process for such dismissals," Sophie pried.

"Bless your heart, honey. We're an employment-at-will state. Employee and employer can end the relationship any time, for any reason, without notice. This law dates back to a master-servant treatise from the late 1800's. Things don't move fast around here."

"The news has spread through the school like wildfire," Bunnie said. "Anne from Personnel processed the severance papers. As for appealing, believe me, they are prepared for these contingencies. He won't be able to sue, and if he tries he'll ruin himself."

"I heard the chief was present at the dismissal. Close like white on rice those two," she added. "I reckon President Holzer needed the extra protection, just in case. You never know what can happen when you wreck someone's life."

"We'll organize and label his research while he's away. Let's have everything ready for him if he comes back. I will miss him. He was a good boss."

The speed at which life could turn toxic depressed Sophie. She turned her thoughts to her friend. Bunnie's job was essential to her survival, losing it would be tragic. She did not have wealthy relatives to call for help. She was alone and unprotected. The thought that something so dreadful could happen to Bunnie frightened her.

Sophie picked up the dishes and set them in the cracked country sink. Everywhere she looked signs of decay were impossible to ignore. She knew that Bunnie, despite her valiant efforts, could not stall the decline of her family home for much longer.

Right after moving in, Sophie had started a list of home improvement projects. They ranged from the ambitious (repair the roof) to the mundane (caulk windows.) She kept the list up until she realized that even the smaller tasks were multiplying out of control. A vast ocean of repairs loomed before them with no land in sight. She knew that Bunnie's entire paycheck disappeared at the local hardware store each month. Her own rent helped pay for food and utilities. There were not enough paint and caulk to fight forty years of neglect.

A knock at the door distracted Sophie from her somber thoughts. She walked to the front parlor and let in David and his little dog, greeting them both with a smile. David was Bunnie's tuner and had taken care of her piano for the past four years. She helped get him the job with the music department and he was now the sole caretaker of a large inventory of grand pianos at Watson. Grateful for the help, he stopped charging Bunnie for her piano tunings soon afterwards.

"How are you ladies doing?" David asked, rolling his heavy tuning case into the house. "Today is a scorcher," he added, accepting a cold glass of sweet tea from Sophie.

"Bless your heart, David; you are in earnest with this restoration! How long do you suppose I'll be without my piano?" Bunnie asked, petting the little Jack Russell.

"I don't want the distraction box to take over my life. These reality shows are pesky."

"I plan to remove the action today and replace the bridle straps next week," David answered, opening his tuning case. He had been working on Bunnie's old piano for the past six months. The proximity to the ocean had a damaging effect on the poor Wurlitzer. It rusted strings and ruined his tunings.

Bunnie and Sophie were laying newspapers on the porch table, preparing for the feast.

"We're having a Lowcountry Boil tonight," Bunnie called out. "I hope you brought your appetite."

David nodded with relish, his stomach growling. He could eat enormous quantities of food and still keep a fit physique. He never left her home without tasting her many signature dishes.

Bunnie was splitting ears of corn on the kitchen counter, recalling the story of the famous stew. "They used to call this meal the Frogmore Stew, but when the post office removed the little hamlet near Beaufort from its register, the stew lost its name. It's called the Lowcountry Boil or Tidewater Boil along the coast."

Sophie had great respect for this one-pot wonder. It had been part of Bunnie's cooking repertoire for decades. It was so easy to make, and healthy to boot, and she loved to entertain with it. With little fuss and maximal impact, Bunnie could feed a crowd of twenty.

She filled a large pot and measured two teaspoons of crab boil spices per quart of water. She brought the broth to a boil and seasoned it. Bunnie added small red potatoes, several links of smoked sausage and let them simmer. A few minutes later, she added the corn.

A ring at the door interrupted her and she rushed to welcome Marie and Isabelle. "So glad you came. Come on in and make yourselves comfortable."

"Mom! Look! She's so cute!" Isabelle squealed, impressed by the little dog's elaborate somersaults.

It took little to put Marie at ease: a smiling host, a friendly dog and the delicious aroma of seafood stew. She felt an instant connection to Bunnie when first meeting her at work. She had accepted her invitation to dinner without a second thought. She delighted in watching Bunnie in her kitchen, surrounded by the enticing aromas of spices. It was impossible to ignore her guest's warmth and welcome.

Marie smiled at kitchens' ability to bring people together. Fellowships long nurtured around campfires and kitchen tables bonded people in primal ways. They came to sustain their bodies and spirits with shared nourishment. Marie fell in with the cooking crowd within minutes and rolled up her sleeves to help.

Isabelle, perched on a stool, was staring at a mound of grey shrimp looking back at her with beady black eyes.

"Mom, look! The shrimp have eyes and antennas! Do we *have* to eat those?" she turned to Bunnie, her eyes aglow with a mix of disgust, fascination, and double-dog-dare fun.

"No sweetie. You can tell a shrimp is fresh by buying it whole. These came in the docks this afternoon, so they are very fresh."

"We usually cook them with heads on, but we'll make an exception tonight," Bunnie winked at the little girl. Isabelle, fascinated by the cooking drama unfolding before her, did not miss a bit.

"We've had some curious culinary adventures since moving here," Marie laughed. "Isabelle had a close call with a hurricane ham stew yesterday. We went to the beach and found sand dollars, knife shells and moon snails. We also saw tear-shaped mounds of sand with tiny funnels gurgling out seawater. We had to find out what laid beneath the surface and we started to dig. Soon, we had gathered a dozen small live conch shells."

"We took a long walk along the shore and met an old man casting three fishing lines into the surf. He was seating on a large cooler cutting up fish in bait-size pieces. Seagulls circled above and sand crabs inspected the cooler and the pile of discarded fish heads," Marie added. "Isabelle showed him her catch. He told us we had all the ingredients for a great hurricane ham stew. We followed his recommendations and steamed the conchs and added okra, green peppers, onion and spices."

"Bless your heart! You didn't make that stew, did you?" Bunnie asked a worried look on her face. "My grandmother spoke of that stew many years ago. But I don't think I've known anyone who's cooked it, let alone ate it. I think that old fisherman may have played a trick on you."

"You may be right. We tried cooking it–without the okra, mind you. The smell was atrocious. The soup resembled a witch's brew. We threw it away," Marie said. She doubted that the smell of her hurricane ham soup could soon fade away from her curtains. She was grateful for Bunnie's good-humored guidance. With such an ally, she may have one up on the locals.

"At least your stew was not as expensive as my wild magnolia purchase," David offered.

"That's true. Marie's story hasn't come close to your magnolia tale," added Sophie daring him to come clean. All eyes on him, David complied.

"I was born and raised in Indiana, and it took me a while to get used to the heavy scents of the south. Everything was new: the pluff mud, the tidal creeks, and the strong perfume of jasmine. It was new to me and I loved it."

"I was looking for a small house and visited several with my real estate agent. She was stunning and witty; a perfect southern belle–she intrigued me. I settled on a ranch house inland, on the river. The broker showed me the house twice, always in the evening. This should have prompted several questions on my part. I did smell a pungent odor I could not place. My agent, in her flirty southern accent, called it the scent of the wild magnolia. It reminded me more of dirty diapers. I discovered, after closing on the house, that the paper mill was less than three miles away. My house was in the path of the famed magnolia bouquet."

"Wild magnolia," added Bunnie with a wink. "We haven't found a story to beat this one, but the hurricane soup is a close second!"

The headless shrimp turned pink and Bunnie ushered her company to the patio. David dumped on the newspaper a smoking mound of hot sausages, shrimp, potatoes, fresh crab and corn on the cob. They sat down and descended on the Lowcountry Boil with abandon.

The heat and humidity slowed the pace of the company gathered around the table. They relished the steam of the last thunderstorms rising from the garden pavers. Bunnie's roses, sated by the downpour, bowed their heads in gratitude. Spanish moss gorged on the afternoon rain swayed from the branches of a majestic live oak. Raindrops scintillated in the setting sun.

The music of Ray Charles echoed in the house. Isabelle napped in the nearby hammock, nestled among pillows with her furry partner. Among such hospitable company, Marie dropped her guard and felt at ease for the first time in months.

The stately mansion, decrepit in the harsh light of day, regained its glory at dusk. The house shed its mantle of decay and under the softening rays of a dying sun shone full of glory once more.

CHAPTER 4
THE LOOKING GLASS

Dinner concluded, the dishes cleaned and put away, Bunnie invited her friends to enjoy the evening breeze on the patio. Assembled around a pitcher of her famous sweet tea and a platter of pecan cookies, the company enjoyed the sound of seagulls cawing in the surf. David watched condensation form on Marie's water glass, wetting her slim fingers. The sight took him back to dark times.

The memories of tumblers, glasses and discarded empty liquor bottles crowded his mind and unsettled him. They often littered his home back in Indiana. He should have known better, protected himself more, and watched out for the signs, but he only saw what he wanted to see.

His new Asian wife had not shown signs of alcoholism during their overseas courtship. He knew she liked to drink, but so did he, and he did not see a problem with it. They got married within a month of their first meeting. The pretense lasted a few months before the pressure of marital life exposed the lie. He had married a promiscuous drunk in need of a green card.

They fought following her nightly binges with her male friends. The fights became more severe, always centering on her need to get booze. His reaction became more intense. Nothing helped. He raided the house daily in search of her cheap whiskey. The hunt, while more thorough, became less productive.

The more intent he was on smoking her out, the more inventive she became at hiding her stash. He knew he was a fool for staying, but she held him close with her sensual games. He felt pathetic and weak but he could not stop wanting her. When he realized she was sharing her bed with others, he began to stir out of his stupor.

A string of humiliating moments brought him back to his senses and to their final confrontation. He had found her stash of alcohol, emptied the bottles, and propped them on the kitchen counter. She came home in the early morning hours, drunk and incensed at his action. The screaming still echoed in his mind. She ran to the kitchen and came back with a carving knife. The deep slash she inflicted on his arm, screaming for her liquor, still seared his psyche.

David woke up from his inertia and called the police. He eventually left his marriage with the shirt on his back and took a job in the Carolinas selling pianos. It had taken him eight long years to get out of his trance.

Marie's glass of water reminded him he had never seen his ex-wife with a glass of water in hand, always liquor. He felt unhinged and restless and excused himself for a smoke on the porch. Tonight was stirring old memories, and he was unsure how to respond. He was calming his nerves with a cigarette when Sophie emerged from the house. She carried a bundle of discarded newspapers, husks, and shells to the compost bin.

Walking back in the house, Sophie noticed David's cigarette glowing in the evening dusk. Mesmerized by the faint glow, she shivered and wrapped her silk shawl on her shoulder. The golden glow of the ashes had conjured up the image of fire and her latest class project. She had been copying a page of the Aberdeen Bestiary.

The fifty-fifth folio featured a mythical bird, which had long fascinated her. With its colorful plumage and majestic gold and scarlet tail, the phoenix inspired her. Its spectacular death and rebirth were integral to her creative process. As an artist and painter, she pushed past conventions. To do so, she needed to burn part of herself and, as a firebird, emerge with new fodder for her art. She envied the phoenix's life expectancy. *What I could do in a millennium,* she mused.

Sophie's presence in the Carolinas was part of this rebirth. Her wish to shed old ways and welcome new experiences was not a reflection on her history; it expressed her curiosity for the future. Raised in a blended family, she had received loving support from her mother, stepfather and brother. They had nurtured her artistic impulses from a young age, accompanying her to auditions and shows.

She began studying fine arts in middle school and could not picture a life without her art. Her mother had taken her to the piers on weekends and let her sketch market scenes since the age of five. The rolling hills and marked seasons of the northeast entranced her. She came from the land of evergreens, red barns and large bales of rolled hay.

Her undergraduate years at Boston School of Arts brought stimulation and heavy workload. Her graduate studies at Watson forced her to change styles and paint new landscapes in new light. Sophie had emerged from her ashes to transition into a new artist. Her passion was melding the new and the old, creating a richer art.

She stopped by the garden to pick up green tomatoes for tomorrow's meal. She returned to the porch and joined Bunnie's guests at the table. She heard David explain to Isabelle the illustrious lineage of his mutt dog and Marie discuss urban renewal with her host. She saw Bunnie's eyes fall on the green tomatoes she dropped on the counter. Without warning, her friend's eyes moistened at the memory of her mother's green fried tomatoes recipe.

Bunnie grew up in the privileged south, oblivious of the racial tension that would birth a civil rights movement. The house was in pristine condition back then. Her siblings were still alive. The house rang with the continuous sounds of family and friends rushing in and out. Her father was still operating the general store and pharmacy he had inherited from his uncle. Her mother kept the family focused on the daily activities of the kitchen and the house. Bunnie remembered the house bigger, cleaner and brighter.

Looking around, she saw the decline and decay eat at her family home. The walls seemed to have shrunk; the paint was peeling and weeds threatened the garden with neglect. The house, maintained with ease by many, had become a financial and emotional burden for one. She doubted she could ever retire and feared she would need to keep working until her death.

"Oh, I've been offered good money for this house but I'm still proud enough of my roots not to go back on my raisin'," Bunnie admitted.

"Yankees, no offense intended, have been buying a piece of the South since the Great Unpleasantness. They have purchased most of the houses on this block. It's a real shame," she added.

Bunnie's house remained one of the few southern strongholds in her neighborhood. It was the most dilapidated one. Gentrification was going rampant throughout the town.

"We need to have a potluck painting party soon," said Sophie. "Get our friends to help on a weekend, after the hurricane season has passed."

"My house survived Gabriella unharmed and it will keep on standing," affirmed Bunnie.

Gabriella was a household name in the South. It had redefined hurricanes in the region for the past twenty years. Sophie soon learned of that storm when moving south. She discovered that one stood on one side or the other of the great Gabriella Divide. You either stood your ground or chose to evacuate. Gabriella was a badge of honor locals were proud to wear and Bunnie was no exception.

"The National Guard came door to door with dog tags."

"Dog tags?" Marie asked.

"For identification," she answered. "They sent no one out during the storm. We were on own. The city deployed their first responders after the hurricane, but it was too late for others."

David remembered the storm. "Gabriella struck during my first year here. We have tornadoes in Indiana but no hurricanes and I didn't know what to expect. I didn't have your grit, Bunnie, and I evacuated a day before the storm. I wrapped up my grand piano, boarded up my house and drove away."

He recalled the hassle of returning home after the storm. "Traffic was impossible. Everyone was in a hurry to check their houses for damages."

"What happened to your home?" Marie wondered.

"The house was fine but debris littered the yard. The storm had uprooted the small shed and wrapped it around my oak tree. And what I remember the most from Gabriella is my bike still perched on its kickstand in the middle of the devastation."

"The water came up six feet at my house," she continued. "I still have the flood marks on the garage walls. The mud in the house covered every surface. It took months to get everything back in order. The storm crushed hundreds of pines and neighborhoods smelled of Pine Sol for months."

"Hurricanes are part of living in the Carolinas," said Bunnie. "Granted, the seasons have been calm for the past five years. We've stayed clear of storms and prayed they'd pass us by and land elsewhere."

"Gabriella was a Category 4 when it landed," added David. "It was one hundred-year storm but don't let that name fool you. It does not mean we are safe for the next eighty years. A hundred-year storm means you have one percent of chance in any hurricane season to get hit. Two of those mega-storms could hit in one year."

"Why do people stay?" Marie asked.

"Some say those who stay are poor. They can't drive, don't have money to leave or are just plain lazy or stupid, but I disagree," Bunnie argued. "I stayed and I'm not stupid or lazy. I loved my house, I had too many pets depending on me, and I believed that God would get me through it, and He did."

As if on cue, three guinea hens, a rooster and five hens approached the table for scraps. Bunnie picked up discarded husks of corn and threw them towards the grateful fowls.

"What can you do when animals depend on you and you can't go to a shelter with a pet goat? What do you do when elder neighbors refuse to go?" she added. "You stay and you ride out the storm, that's what you do. You stay and you pray."

Marie, who had spent the past two years running away from everything, felt humbled by such true grit.

Bunnie's mix of southern wisdom and confederate resilience was a remarkable sight. Holding court in her decaying mansion, Bunnie endured. Her valiant efforts at rebuking old age impressed Marie. Bunnie will one day lose the battle but she still had much to give. She fought as many southerners had done before–for God and family, for life and for land.

CHAPTER 5

THE ACORN

Sophie and Bunnie wasted no time in removing Dr. Wilson's documents from the school. Between both their cars, they had twelve boxes to organize and ship to Atlanta. News had been brief. John's son had taken him in and was selling his house to make the move permanent.

"He is not thinking of his awards and frames now, but he may one day," Bunnie said. "We'll send his affairs from the school's mailroom. That is the least they can do for him. Once the dust settles, he will be glad to have his research."

They spent the night organizing dossiers. They were packing the boxes by country and era.

"President Holzer dropped by this morning looking for you," Sophie warned her friend. "He was searching for documents we brought home with us last Friday. I feigned ignorance."

"He's been insistent. I have avoided him until we can get through the files ourselves and figure out what he wants. We owe Dr. Wilson that much," she added.

"He sure likes to carry on with this foolishness. These hurricane exercises have whipped the departments into frenzy. One more drill and I quit!" Bunnie snapped.

"Last time I checked, Hanna was still barreling towards Miami," Sophie ventured, trying to appease her friend.

"Look at this," Bunnie said, brandishing a box of trash bags. "His plan is laudable–as if the flimsy things could protect the equipment. It's as useful as a trapdoor on a canoe!"

"Good thing we are on break. Imagine the pandemonium if classes were still in session, "said Sophie.

Marie walked into the office, a file in hand, and a question on her mind.

"Ladies, I'm trying to authenticate several ancient bills of sales from an Italian estate for President Holzer. I don't understand the urgency of this, but I need to do more research. Could you please show me the archives?"

Bunnie ushered Marie through the door with a wink at Sophie. "Follow me, I'll take you there. We call it the Maze."

They walked past hallways and storage rooms, canvas slots, studios, metal and wood shops. The archival room was in the basement of the building and housed important documents.

A key in hand, Bunnie opened the door when a movement caught her eye.

"Why don't you go ahead Dr. Caldwell? I saw something moving over there. I'll see who's lurking in the shadows."

Marie entered the Maze and left her to investigate. She smiled at Bunnie's wish to follow protocol and not show undue familiarity at work. She could see the logic in it. It allowed them to keep their relationship private from President Holzer.

Bunnie continued to the furnace room, which contained two entryways. The maintenance crew used one door and condemned the other. Her seniority at school had advantages. She picked up a set of keys, selected the right key and opened the door. She searched the space to no avail. It was empty. Still shaking her head, she returned to Marie who was lost among a pile of papers.

"I saw someone, a shadow, hurry along that corridor and disappear. I don't know where he went."

"He?" asked Marie.

"Yes, it was just a feeling. I saw slacks and not a skirt."

"The campus is old and this building is older," joined in Marie. "We've only scratched the surface. We have many places to explore and documents to scan. I couldn't find an inventory database anywhere to catalog our research."

Marie rummaged through the open filing cabinets to no avail. "I can't even locate the Renaissance files referenced in this folder."

"They may be among Dr. Wilson's papers. He was messy; but he knew where everything was. If this file is there we'll find it."

"Will your home be OK?" Marie asked, thinking of the approaching storm and switching to more important matters.

Bunnie laughed, dismissing her concern. "David and Sophie have helped shore up the house. They even scheduled a painting party next month."

"His piano work isn't enough?"

Bunnie's smile brightened her face. "No. He has a soft spot for seniors on limited income. He is always repairing something. I feed him and he takes it as payment. I suspect he is lonesome when he gets home. His big excuse now is to prepare my house for the season."

"You are a native, Bunnie. Aren't you worried?"

"Not yet. The storm is expected to head to Florida. We may get tropical strength winds when she makes it up the coast, nothing more."

"Why don't you drop by this evening for grilled shrimp and collard greens?" Bunnie offered. "Sophie and David are helping me prepare for the hurricane season. My neighbor's son has brought over ten pounds of wild-caught shrimp. It's 'all you can eat' tonight!"

"Thank you for the invitation," answered Marie, beaming. "Isabelle loves your house, your pets and David's little dog. I, for one, enjoy your great cooking and the company. Let me know what to bring. Maybe we can search for those missing letters and stay a step ahead of President Holzer."

Bunnie picked up her purse, stood up and mumbled under her breath something about a 'knee-high' and a 'grasshopper,' and was gone.

Shortly after returning home with Isabelle, Marie changed and walked along the short street leading to Bunnie's house. She was holding Isabelle's hand and listening to her adventures. The second day at school had proved more exciting. Isabelle had now two best friends, and a homeroom teacher she liked. Her first *Show and Tell* had been a success, given kids' penchant for things gross and despicable.

"They loved my hurricane stew story. Too bad, I had no leftovers to bring!"

"That's a good thing," Marie laughed. "You don't want them to evacuate the school."

She smiled at all the positive changes the Carolinas had brought to her daughter.

Isabelle had transitioned to her surroundings better than she could have hoped. *Give a kid a tree house and a tiny furry companion, and the world brightens up,* she thought. David's dog had a soothing effect on Isabelle. Marie was now considering getting a puppy to cement the bond with their new home.

Isabelle had lost her haunted look of the past two years. The first six months were the hardest, with her family walking on eggshells around them both. Unable to express sorrow in front of a bereaved eight-year old, they pretended nothing was wrong.

Marie looked around the room in gratitude. So much has changed in a year. She was lucky for such friends. Bunnie, eccentric and imperious, ruled her roost with the panache of a theater director. Sophie's paintings displayed true talent, scope and breath of work for one so young. David was a welcome relief from the strings of men who wanted to date her since she came out of mourning.

She remembered the disastrous blind date her brother had set her on. She had since refused to date. Life was far simpler that way. David *was* a good-looking man, with muscular shoulders, a mane of golden hair and blue eyes showing great care and compassion. He was friendly, but not familiar, considerate without being overbearing. Maybe they could become friends. Marie could offer little else.

She looked at her daughter and exhaled for the first time in ages. She lacked the buoyancy of childhood and yearned for the resilience of youth. While Isabelle's night terrors subsided within six months of the accident, hers still endured.

She often experienced the same relentless and terrifying dream, chased by a light along a tunnel. Hands stapled to the walls grabbed her clothes and scratched her face and arms, tearing her apart. A year of therapy had blunted the edges of the nightmare without erasing the torment it stirred in her mind.

The secret hid at the center, burrowing deeper in unfathomable places, out of reach. Marie knew she had precious little time before the secret disappeared, hidden from sight forever.

Leaving the northeast had been her first courageous act in two years. It was not, as her family feared, an escape from reality but an attempt to face her demons alone. Sitting in Bunnie's kitchen, the task proved less daunting and more hopeful and interesting.

On the counter sat a large antique milk glass bowl filled to the brim with shelled jumbo shrimp. Since tasting her first Lowcountry Boil, Marie knew them to be firmer and healthier. They spent their short lives swimming in the ocean, instead of diseased ponds overseas. Marie was a convert. She gave up farm-raised for wild-caught during her first meal at Bunnie's.

Standing by the sink, Sophie squeezed the juice of two plump lemons on the shrimp. She dusted them with a generous helping of Old Bay seasonings and a few shakes of pink salt. Marie approached the table and began skewering the shrimp. Outside, David had started the grill and oiled the grates. Bunnie grabbed a mound of collard greens and dropped them in a large pan. The smells of caramelized onions, greens and bacon ignited the kitchen with mouth-watering smells.

Isabelle carried plates and napkins to the porch, followed by her new white shadow. Doodle showed off elaborate begging routines with great panache and success.

"Hope springs eternal with that one," David laughed, bringing along the platter of grilled shrimp.

"It's such a simple way to prepare them," Bunnie said. "You can't go wrong when you have the best cooking ingredients and a blessing."

"A blessing?" Marie asked.

"Each year, our community celebrates the Blessing of the Fleet to honor our small group of shrimpers. You must have seen the docks and boats moored by the creek. Our shrimping fleet has dwindled to a shadow of what it used to be. We have lost two-thirds of the boats over the past three decades and less than ten trawlers now make a living from the sea. Each year, a priest blesses the boats during a ceremony at the start of the shrimping season."

"The sea captains wage a battle against an onslaught of overseas shrimp. Our shrimpers need our blessings before setting out to sea each spring," she added.

Until her first taste of wild-caught shrimp, Marie had dined in ignorance.

"They feel blessed," Marie said, taking a mouthful of pink crustacean and agreed. "They're delicious!"

The conversation ebbed and flowed. The food was fresh, delicious and simple. Old Bay seasoning was a staple of Bunnie's cooking dusted on most everything–fish, meat and chicken.

Bunnie knew everyone in town. She had spent decades nurturing her contacts. She helped neighbors with their kids' college applications and friends with their resumes. In return, local shrimpers made sure she was never without shrimp or clams. Bunnie was a neighborhood treasure, a communal project. David had fallen under the same spell and volunteered for food and company.

"How far along are you with the window repairs?" Sophie asked him.

"I've cut the plywood to cover the windows and pre-drilled holes. That will make the installation easy before a storm."

"Bless your heart!" Bunnie replied with a piece of cornbread in one hand and a fork of collard greens in the other.

"Masking tape isn't enough, then?"

"Taping large X's on your windows will cause more damage," Bunnie answered. "Mrs. Manigault swears by it, but I don't. Instead of having small fragments of glass, you have larger chards stuck to the tape, creating deadlier flying projectiles in the house."

"Boards are what you need," David said looking at Marie. "I will build shutters for your home too."

Distracted by the activity in the yard, Marie observed various animals enjoying their evening meal. Birds and squirrels battled over several birdbaths and feeders. Three fat cats lounged on old wooden rocking chairs, casting lazy glances at the guests before ignoring them. Anxious guinea hens patrolled the grounds in military formations, keeping the perimeter secure. A dozen gnomes, in various states of peeling, marked the path leading to the chicken coop. She followed a trail of bleached conch shells to the vegetable garden. It linked the rabbit coop to Rosalie's enclosure where the white goat grazed on nutritious weeds.

Bunnie is right to take responsibility for her little zoo, Marie thought. They depended on her for their sustenance and where could you evacuate a goat? Marie, who was only responsible for her daughter, felt overwhelmed with the logistics of such venture.

They finished the meal in comfortable silence, enjoying the view and the summer fare. They saw the weather turn and the cover of clouds approach. Soon, a summer storm was upon them, releasing torrential rain on the parched earth. Thunder and lightning tore the sky apart and unleashed a dramatic sight of sound and light. From the comfort of their covered porch, Bunnie and her guests enjoyed the deluge. The rain washed away heat and dust and chased three indignant cats inside the house.

The dishes done and put away, Sophie picked at the files stacked in boxes along the wall. She had finished reviewing the French files and was starting the Italian one. Marie, who was helping her, noticed a familiar name–Villa Criccoli.

The same name was in the files she had researched for President Holzer. She looked at the ancient bills of sale with newfound interest. What did Villa Criccoli have in common with a list of renaissance household items listed on the old receipt?

"Let's set aside the documents referencing a Villa Criccoli. We have several items purchased by Dr. Wilson. They are in storage in several buildings across campus."

"Why are those files important to President Holzer?" asked Sophie, waving a bunch of papers in front of her.

Marie opened a folder, glancing at the content with renewed interest. "I don't know, but we'll figure out the connection." President Holzer's growing obsession with the authentication papers started to unhinge her.

"Something *is* amiss," Bunnie hinted, perched on her rickety rocking chair. "I saw someone disappear into the furnace room. Horace, the maintenance man, could not open the door. So, I've asked Melanie in Buildings and Grounds to help locate the key to the second door. Even a blind hog finds an acorn now and then!"

"The furnace room, near the auditorium?" David asked.

"Yes," she answered. "The one next to the stage. It lets out a clunking sound now and then during performances."

"I saw President Holzer come out of that room this afternoon," David added. "I was tuning a piano and I startled him. He looked upset to see me."

CHAPTER 6

THE VAULT

His discovery was better than anything he had ever experienced. It was more exciting than his power plays at school. It was more exquisite than a single Highland malt scotch maturing for decades in a Scottish distillery. It was more rousing than his recent sexual marathon with a young sophomore. It defied the mind and captured the imagination.

Charles caressed the smooth marble piece in an intimate exchange with its creator. His find could shatter established beliefs and crush academic reputations. On the other hand, it could stay hidden in his house, a well-guarded secret. People would kill to own this most remarkable object and that fact aroused him.

It came to a startling revelation last year when the proof crashed on his desk. He deserved this marvel. He alone had gathered the evidence and looked for confirmation in forgotten places. Luck had its place, he admitted. You did not stumble upon such a discovery without the touch of the Gods.

Charles felt vindicated in firing John. Given enough time and academic curiosity, his colleague might have solved the puzzle. What he needed to do now was tie loose ends and complete the authentication process. No copies of the letters existed in the boxes he removed from John's office. The secretary must have retained some documents.

His original plan had been to put the sculpture on the black market and retire with a fortune. Yet, holding such a unique piece of history, such a twist on the past, captivated him. *Why sell it?* It was the most exquisite thing he had ever possessed. *Why share it with anyone?* He was already wealthy.

A brisk knock at the door interrupted his reveries. His new hire entered, smiling and ready to brief him on her first week at work. He remarked on her good looks again. Distracted by his own musings, he perked up when she mentioned the authentication papers.

"I cannot authenticate these Italian letters until I view the originals," she insisted, her tone grating at him.

"Don't bother with this. We need your signature as acting director. It's just a formality."

"It may well be, but I cannot attest to something I have not seen. I must study the documents and offer an opinion."

"You don't have time," Charles interrupted, cutting short his pretense at affability. "This is your first priority. I have my plate full with hurricane preparations and can't babysit you on this."

"Babysitting will not be necessary," Marie snapped back, offended by his attitude.

Charles watched her walk out of his office and knew that she wouldn't pass probation. She was charming enough, even stunning, with her raven hair, green eyes, and slender body; but she was too headstrong. He needed to get rid of her, soon.

Back at his desk, he turned his thoughts to a more pressing matter. The hurricane was now set to hit the lower Carolinas. He had not conducted an emergency preparedness drill for the past two years and admitted it was long overdue. *I've grown complacent,* he realized.

Not a single landfall had rattled residents or the media since Gabriella. The flurry of storms followed a similar route in the middle of the Atlantic. A few hurricanes had even veered toward Europe. This extended peaceful hurricane season lulled newcomers in a false sense of security. Inactivity dulled the response to the danger. It was time to set up an emergency preparedness drill and get his staff motivated again.

The new student center was built to code and could withstand extreme weather. The century-old fine arts building and most of the dorms could not survive a large hurricane. With most of the students on break, the president contacted the police chief with instructions to hold a drill the following day. The exercise served two purposes and allowed him to test Watson's readiness and his own ability to protect his treasure.

Over the years, Charles' collection had grown from good to exquisite. He found in the school's forgotten rooms a delightful playground to feed his passion. The university had gained dozens of first-class paintings over the past century. The pieces, inventoried and stored, had passed hands and some had vanished in storage, for lack of proper identification. While it disappeared from the museum's inventory and ceased to exist in the school's databases, the art survived in Charles's collection.

The university was his playground. Attics, basements, and old things fascinated him. His attention to detail helped him see order where others saw chaos. This gift helped him amass a beautiful collection on the school's dime. He waited for employees to move to other jobs or retire, for memories to fail. He alone knew of the lost paintings.

Charles was not afraid of exposure. His public persona was deeply entrenched in the good graces of the Board. His job was to protect Watson, and he did so with meticulous care. The university had lived through high and low points. It had notably discriminated against black students seeking entry into the school. Yet, it was the first college in the state to hire a black female professor. Its story was one of contradictions.

When hired, Charles labored to smooth and enhance the school's reputation. His favorite tactics included manipulation, intimidation and fear. He controlled information to meet his needs. The Watson Board of Directors soon gave him free rein as long as he met deadlines, goals and objectives. He always did. He knew the scandals, small and large, that had occurred during his tenure and had squashed them all. The Board, in turn, rewarded him for his vigilance and for his ability to prevent and diffuse problems.

His mind racing to the present, Charles realized he had to find a secure location for his art. The curator's secured storage was too obvious and regulated, each piece found at the touch of a button. The risk of exposure was too high within the museum and prompted him to hide his art at home. He alone recognized their intrinsic worth and need to preserve them. Over the years, his role of steward evolved to that of rightful owner. Stewardship became ownership. He could not imagine parting from them.

Over the past decades, Charles discovered a maze of tunnels below the school connecting to the oldest buildings. Few, if any, knew of their existence. He never solved their original purpose despite his study of the historical record. What surprised him most was that someone decided so long ago to dig and set up a deep maze of underground burrows. Basements are uncommon in the coastal south and highly unpractical. Sea level conditions make them prone to hurricanes, tidal movement and storm surges. Yet, a prior school president had judged it important enough to build a web of passageways to evade detection. One of Watson's founding fathers had, for reasons long forgotten, preferred to keep them secret.

Charles had protected the same secret for the better part of his tenure. He kept the maintenance crew busy, away from the underground structures. In the few instances when he had to shore up the channel or mend a brick wall, he called for outside help. A discreet company from New York always performed the repairs.

The president's house connected to the art building by one of those long-forgotten tunnels. A tunnel that now proved useful in moving paintings from dusty storage rooms to his house–a silent partner in his quest to preserve his art. Hanna was providing him with a reason to execute his own drill.

Charles left his office, walked home to pick up two keys and hurried to the basement. On the south wall, behind the furnace and storage shelves, he had installed a steel door. Punching numbers on the keypad, he heard the pins disengage and walked into a much older part of the underpass. A second forged iron gate blocked his way, but the turn of an antique key soon let him through. He always relished his descent into the darkness.

The tunnel leading to the art building had never been wired for light. Not wishing to call attention to his comings and goings, Charles had kept it a secret. He walked through the maze in complete obscurity, relying on his knowledge of the place to take him to Franklin. The passageway, built with local bricks produced on nearby plantations, was a great ally. A distinctive aroma of earth and humidity permeated the air. Water leaked in perpetual gloom keeping the walls damp and musty. The effect was that of entering a preternatural cave.

Charles loved his tunnel. It provided him privacy and a secure way to the school. While he had mapped the better part of the maze, the passageway to Franklin was the only one he used. It allowed him to travel from one building to the next in less than ten minutes. The president closed the door and entered a maintenance room only he had access. He dialed a combination and gained entrance. An antique floor safe stood in the middle of the room.

He had discovered it a decade ago and still remembered the thrill of the hunt. His mind, back then, was abuzz with possibilities. What treasure awaited him? He had whipped himself into a frenzy trying to open it and spent months studying techniques to crack the vault. The less invasive method was to jimmy the lock, but serrated wheels within it made it hard to break.

He spent nights and weeks trying to unlock the safe. He could have walked into the art building through the front door and reached the vault with ease, but Charles preferred the thrill of the game and the joy of anonymity. The tunnels and the safe were his secrets to keep.

He considered picking and even drilling the lock. He spent hours studying drill-point diagrams, but could not take such a radical step. To do so would expose him to undue scrutiny.

Dynamite, as tempting as it was by then to his frazzled brain, was out of the question. Charles knew that a safe was only as secure as its combination. After a restless evening, he walked to the vault at midnight and stood in the darkness. He had spent countless hours studying the 1895 British model, and poured over the history of the English models ad nauseam. While his research had taken him to England, it was home that he found the answer.

Charles directed his thoughts to America and to the Carolinas. The dampness of the walls, the eerie ambiance of the tunnel, and the tragic loss of teenage sons conjured up the War Between the States. He recalled the many expressions used to describe the Civil War. Soon the ghosts of young men rose before him eager to enlist in a conflict that would bring the South to its knees. A litany of desolate moments came to mind.

Charles tried several combinations, dates of battles and significant events, with no luck. Exhausted, he closed his eyes and conjured up fallen brothers. He inhaled and dialed 5-1-1-1-2. The lock disengaged. His heart skipped a few beats; he exhaled and took a step forward to open the vault.

CHAPTER 7

THE WRAP AROUND PORCH

"We're looking for a black cat in a coal cellar," Bunnie complained. She was preparing her famous mustard sauce for the pulled pork she planned to serve for dinner. Sophie sat on the sofa, immersed in a stack of papers. She was scanning a pile of documents with a portable digital wand before entering them into a computer database.

"We might as well digitize every notable piece of paper now. It will help with the search," Marie pointed the boxes still lining up the wall of the hallway.

She could hear hammering on the porch. David was drilling several thick planks of plywood he planned to affix to the windows before a potential hurricane landfall. Isabelle and Dood kept him company. Wind and surge were the biggest enemies during a storm, he had told them. Bunnie's large bay windows were an inviting mean of entry and needed to be boarded.

Five years ago, Bunnie had moved her sleeping quarters to the more convivial downstairs parlor. She grew tired of playing the part of a lonesome Scarlett in an empty and crumbling Tara. When she opened her home to her friend and boarder, she offered Sophie her bedroom. It was the largest room, facing south, with a forged iron balcony gilded by a canopy of wisterias. She often reflected on her choice with satisfaction. Sophie could spend hours at the window, painting, observing and meditating. *The house had found a new belle,* Bunnie thought.

Within a few weeks of moving in, Sophie understood Bunnie's predicament. The house was a delight of exquisite architecture and artisanship in dire need of repair. In an age of prefabricated and modular construction, Bunnie's home was a splendid reminder of a bygone era.

A few months ago, Sophie sized up the three unoccupied upstairs bedrooms and thought of a way to help Bunnie's besieged life. She enlisted David in convincing her stubborn roommate to agree to her plan. Together, they suggested renting out the remaining rooms to responsible graduate students. David could strip the walls, caulk the windows and fix the bathrooms; she could apply a fresh coat of paint to the rooms. Sophie smiled and knew she had won a battle. Her studies at Watson would end someday and she wanted to leave Bunnie with a stable income to retire.

"Bunnie has allowed us to fix the rooms upstairs," she whispered to David, unable to contain her excitement. David took off his weathered work gloves and set them aside next to his tools.

"You've got to be kidding! I will pick up wallpaper stripper, paint and caulk at the store before she changes her mind. We can get the bedrooms ready by the time spring session begins."

Before they could firm up plans, their genteel southern belle appeared in the living room ringing the bell for dinner.

"I'm fixing to bring the last dish to the table," she announced. "Why don't y'all freshen up before joining me on the porch?"

Outdoor entertaining was a treat this time of year. The warmth of the garden, the crackle of the thunderstorms, and the scent of the rain on the fresh cut grass were inviting. Everyone converged to the porch as the heavens opened and released their soothing rain. The effect was instantaneous on the flock of clucking guinea hens, rushing under the sheds in flapping protest.

The company sat at the table and began their meal in silence, listening to the rain. They savored meat they knew had fallen off the bone a few hours ago. The sauce, tangy with a hint of sweetness, coated the pulled pork with a Carolina twist.

"Thank you for working so hard, David. We might yet be ready for Hanna," Bunnie said passing the butter pickles. "She veered north last night. They are saying Georgia and South Carolina might be next. We should be fine, but it never hurts to be ready. This one is too early to call."

Marie listened to the hurricane tales with growing anxiety and dismay. She had carefully planned her move after a persistent courtship from Watson. She chose the right middle school for Isabelle and a perfect house in a quaint neighborhood with a sense of history. She planned for multiple emergencies, but she never thought of hurricanes. She had laid the groundwork for a solid and stable world for her daughter. This world was now growing murky and uncertain with each weather forecast. Marie always planned for the worst since the accident, life had taught her that much. Yet, she sensed something amiss in the dismal of Dr. Wilson and her abrupt promotion. Now this hurricane looming in the Atlantic further unsettled her.

She felt the pull of the tide tearing her in a new direction. Walls rose from the confines of her mind, pulled from the vast pool of darkness hiding within her. The walls always came up, casting a protective spell over her and her daughter. Hurricane Hanna proved to be the allegory that best described the imponderability of life.

Despite her best efforts to build a safety zone around her child, they were now facing a hurricane!

Hanna inched up the coast with every status update. The new calculations projected her to make landfall in Charleston, South Carolina. The storm had grown from a wave off the Cape Verde Islands to a catastrophic storm. Marie was new to this world. The word hurricane kept on creeping up with every conversation. The break room was abuzz with advice.

For someone averse to risk, Marie was at a loss to understand her choice. She could not recall discussing hurricanes with her real estate agent. The lull in hurricane strikes on the East Coast had wiped the threat from the news. Hurricanes had never crossed her mind while planning her move, but they now occupied her daily thoughts.

The news stations bombarded listeners with tips on how to prepare for the storm. Marie knew to drive several hours inland to locate a safe place. Her disaster supplies kit was at the ready, enough gas, and no pets to board. David had picked up extra gallons of water at the store this morning. She had placed her valuables and personal papers in waterproof containers and purchased a new flashlight and batteries. Marie could handle the slow pace and predictability of a hurricane. They planned to be long gone before Hanna slammed the coast. Yet, Marie understood what had prompted Bunnie to stay behind and take care of stranded humans and fowls. An umbrella large enough to protect Bunnie and friends did not exist. Only an act of God could.

"Have you found a clue?" David asked, noting Marie's unease and pointing to the stack of papers before her. He knew the distracting power of a good mystery.

"Not yet," Marie answered. "But President Holzer's mounting frustration tells me we're getting close."

"He hasn't found them and neither have we. The demise of Dr. Wilson must be connected to this hunt. The clue's got to be here," Bunnie agreed, pointing to the mass of papers.

"You catalogued the French files. I scanned the files on High Renaissance Florence," Sophie added. "We're getting close."

"Florence," Bunnie recalled. "What a lovely city! The study abroad with the students and Dr. Wilson was a trip of a lifetime."

They turned in unison and faced Bunnie. "You were in Florence with Dr. Wilson?" Marie asked.

"Yes, five years ago, chaperoning a dozen students."

"Did you spend much time with Dr. Wilson in Florence?" asked Sophie.

"No, we didn't. He spent much of his time at country estate auctions or meeting with colleagues and contacts. We never saw him, but he had a knack for bringing back home the best artifacts for the school. I remember ushering the students through customs on the way back home. We waited for hours for Dr. Wilson and his curiosities."

"What was he doing? "David asked.

"He was bringing back several white marble pieces from a sculptor in Carrara. There were two crates from an estate auction near Barberino-something," continued Bunnie.

"Barberino di Mugello?" Marie asked.

"Yes, I believe it was. The name sounds right. Italian customs detained us until they could verify our purchases. The Italians don't appreciate the theft of their historical heritage," Bunnie winked.

Sophie reached for a folder. "That name is familiar. I looked at a file containing that summer's purchases."

Bunnie continued to reminisce. "We had our conference on the grounds of the Villa Medici at Cafaggiolo. Dr. Wilson bought several Maiolica pieces there."

"Maiolica?" David asked, his art history classes a vague memory.

"Yes, tin-glazed earthenware. Artisans produced this popular pottery at Cafaggiolo in 1495 under the patronage of the Medicis. They called the potteries 'painted with stories'," Marie explained.

"How is this helping us?" David asked.

"President Holzer is looking to authenticate the Florentine papers," Marie realized, looking at her friends.

"And Dr. Wilson, who favored France, only visited Italy once. We are searching for Italian letters connected to him," Sophie added.

The excitement was palpable when they realized they had found a major clue. The puzzle was taking shape and was leading them to fifteenth-century Florence.

"It's got to be here. The entire content of the Italian summer trip is in the box," said Bunnie riffling through the folders. "Receipts, catalogs, letters, research papers. I did not think of looking there. These are housekeeping files."

"The Maiolica pieces are in the Renaissance Wing of the museum," she added. "I don't know what happened to the marble pieces."

Silence settled in the room, more indictment than defense. Bunnie glimpsed at her friends and saw the same look of reserved opinion.

"Are you implying that Dr. Wilson did something nefarious?" Bunnie asked. "Dr. Wilson was honest in his dealings with the school. He was meticulous in his reimbursements and documented his purchases to the penny. He never took long lunches or charged the school for personal items."

"Why did he get fired, then?" David asked.

Marie stood up, ready to bring the dishes to the kitchen, looking at her friends. This riddle concerned them as much as it perplexed her. "That's what we'll find out because none of this firing and hiring makes any sense. Something has happened and Dr. Wilson holds the key."

"He is under observation at the hospital and unable to answer our questions," Bunnie reminded them. "We will have to solve this riddle ourselves."

CHAPTER 8
THE SENATOR

Charles still recalled the day he opened the vault. A sweep of his flashlight had exposed a vacant safe, musty and damp and unleashed a world of frustration. He had built such anticipation around the discovery that a possible failure never occurred to him. The memory still hurt after all these years. He learned to forget the humiliating sting of the vault, but not its existence. When time came to preserve his growing collection, he turned to the perfect place and filled it with his treasures.

The impending storm, oppressive and sinister, loomed large over his peace of mind. The projected track, inching along the East Coast, had not yet settled on a specific path, but he could not wait for Hanna to make up her mind.

Charles marched through the familiar tunnel holding two wrapped paintings. He performed his own emergency preparedness exercise with precision, clocking the time he took to move his collection to the safe. His art was in jeopardy. To lose what he had spent fifteen years collecting was unthinkable. They had not evacuated the school once during his tenure and the chance for a direct hit increased with each passing year. The vault, while an early source of displeasure, proved serendipitous when fighting a hurricane.

Charles transported and lined dozens of pieces in the safe within an hour. He stacked protective casings and Styrofoam boxes next to leather portfolios. He smiled–his safe was no longer empty but packed with his life's worth. His collection, amassed over the past decade, had begun with a serendipitous find. In a push to automate the art inventory of the school, he had noticed discrepancies. Not every painting had complete custody records, making its identification problematic. In less than a year, he had collected two dozen unclaimed pieces ranging from minor to major works. He adopted forgotten pictures that had long ago disappeared from Watson's memory.

His first acquisition was a watercolor by society portraitist John Singer Sargent. He remembered dusting off the small object in Franklin's basement. Someone had the foresight to pack the image in sturdy cloth. Peeling off the layers of time and neglect, he uncovered a brilliant landscape. The quarried hills of Carrara shone in the darkness. The artistry of the painter had evolved from his notorious oil portraits to evocative landscapes. Luminous and radiant, the painting ignited his passion. Smitten with his first find, Charles launched his quest. The treasure hunt began with the Carrara watercolor and continued for a decade through the dark corners of the school. He left no attic unexamined, no basement unexplored. In doing so, he found small and large pieces abandoned in the bowels of the older buildings.

The president's plan was simple: build his collection, sell a portion and retire to Italy with the art he could not part with. Charles had fallen madly in love with Tuscany during his graduate studies and never wavered in his devotion. His aspiration to live in such an artistic and breathtaking region only grew stronger. He began preparing his exit from academia a decade ago. His family wealth had provided a solid base from which to gain independence, but he needed more assets to insure a life of permanent ease. He was planning his retirement, using the resources of the school to help him transition to a new world. His Italian was fluent and his political understanding of the culture kept fresh with doses of La Nazione and the Florentine. Charles had restored a stunning property in Tuscany he had recently purchased. He was ready to move his art and start a new life overseas.

His heart dreamt of Italy but his paranoia anchored him at Watson. The school must never know of the paintings it had abandoned to neglect and obscurity. To wrap up loose ends before his departure, Charles remained focused on finding the perfect blind replacement.

He grew irritated thinking of Dr. Caldwell. The authentication of the papers was essential to making a clean break. She had not proven malleable. He sensed an obstinate temperament he could not manipulate. However, she was a widow with a young child, in a new town, without connections, alliances or support. Her time at Watson would be short.

He turned his thoughts back to his art. Several pieces of white marble, packed and stacked on a dolly, awaited transport and marked his last trip to the vault. He cherished holding onto the secrets of this famous sculptor. Experts and scholars had written much on the artist without unveiling the depth and breadth of his life experience. Charles felt a deep affinity with the master. They both had persevered, walked the path less traveled and struggled to express their passions. Charles related to the toil both had endured to craft their private and public personae. The dreariness of his administrative duties mirrored the Florentine artist's obligations. Both sought financial liberation from modern board members or Renaissance patrons.

The ignorant and the blind populated the world today as they did during the Dark Ages. He would have given everything to be part of the birth of Renaissance. An entire continent engaged in the fire of creation. It was a time when art, if labeled sacrilegious, was punishable by excommunication and death. It was the age of champions, patrons and protectors. Charles hated the expression *art for the masses.* Masses could not comprehend the breath, depth and communion the arts exalted in his soul. His move to Florence was the escape from the mundane, the dreariness and the vapid.

He yearned to walk along Borgo Santi Apostoli on the smooth stones polished to a satin glow by the steps of countless visitors. The coolness of the little Piazza del Limbo and the gelato store off the Piazza de Santa Trinita delighted him. He longed to sit on the steps of Il Duomo where five hundred years before Platonists held spirited debates. Florence still held the imprint of artistic giants. Tuscan light breathed life in every corner of its medieval streets.

Charles enjoyed living with history and the constant brush with revenants. He saw the ghost of Savonarola burning at the stake on Santa Maria de la Novella's public place. He witnessed David, the symbol of the Florentine heart, standing guard over the Piazza de la Signoria. He heard Dante's steps echoing into the darkness. He recognized the mad spirit of Botticelli throwing his work in the Bonfire of the Vanities. Charles loved the drama, blood and tears the old stones conjured up. The trace of history, captured in the shavings of a string instrument, sung to him. He savored it in the *trattorias* surrounding Il Duomo, in the warmth of the sun on the colored marble. Six more months and he would embrace a world that beheld art at an instinctive and visceral level. He longed to return the Italian maestro to the center of his new home.

Charles realized this defining moment began in childhood. He had never played or shared well with others. Far from being a flaw, he credited his natural impulse for his success. An only child, he never endured fights with siblings or the divided attention of his parents. His father, a career politician, taught him to conceal his true self with a sterling public image.

In his pursuit of influence and power, Senator Henri Holzer never lost sight of the end game. His campaigns trumpeted a political promise he never intended to keep. He sold dreams, feelings and illusions. A good elected official, he had an acute perception of human frailties and a flair for the stage. Remarkably, he struck partnerships that continued to help his heir a decade after his death. Henry's connections had secured Charles' position at Watson. His family pedigree was an integral part of his public persona.

Henri Holzer taught his son to be ruthless, driven and focused in the pursuit of his bliss. Yet, what the senator held sacred had little hold over his son. Unlike the father who pursued wealth and influence, the only son's true passions were more exotic. He enjoyed comfort but did not mistake it for an end. His obsession was with the exquisite. His delights were in possessing the exceptional, the superb and the magnificent.

In his Tuscan villa, Charles planned to surround himself with his art and live a life examined. He knew the sacrifices the maestro endured to reach his goal. There were uncomprehending patrons, inept commissions and demeaning competitive purses in High Renaissance. He felt no less alienated in his modern era.

The world oppressed him; forces prompted him to reexamine his choices. The small figure of a long-abandoned child, his child, stood in the darkness. He had severed relations with his wife years ago. He could not expose his expanding collection to curious eyes. A Cassatt, a Monet, and two Picassos had followed the discovery of the Sargent watercolor. His collection was growing and could not pass for copies to his companion.

His ex-wife had spent her graduate studies at the Louvre as a copyist. She was an art insurer with a prestigious firm whose presence in his life was too dangerous. Charles did not hesitate when it came time to choose between his obligations and his passions. He severed relations with his wife and daughter long ago and only spoke to them through lawyers.

He had dismissed his child until now. His love for his collection had grown and with it the need to curate and preserve it. He had no succession plan, no legacy, no one to protect his life's work after his death. He thought of donating his collection anonymously, but an entrepreneurial journalist may still track its provenance and expose his actions. Charles was the guardian of his family history and could not smear it with a scandal.

Hanna unnerved him. His collection, vulnerable and at the mercy of the elements, presented him with few practical options. He could ill-afford to insure it, and he could not bear to move it off-site while staying on the premises. The vault was a providential find, but he still felt his collection imperiled. The storm was getting closer and could prove catastrophic. Charles had called local rental truck companies without success. None was available. He resigned himself to standing guard through the hurricane.

A third of his paintings were in the hands of black-market collectors in America. His contact assured him the demand was still high on this side of the Atlantic. He had sold the expendable part of his collection to wealthy American patrons. The proceeds set aside in an offshore account were enough to transition comfortably to Florence. Charles planned to book the rest of his art on a transatlantic passage with contacts in the ports of Charleston and Le Havre to aid with transport. The move of his collection to Italy was testing his resolve. He chased the bile of stress with visions of Florence in the spring. He saw himself sitting on the terrace of his villa, sipping a glass of Vernaccia di San Gimignano. The success of his venture depended on how methodical and precise his departure would be. No loose ends, no damning documents, no witness. *Fortes fortuna iuvat,* he thought, closing the door of his vault. *Fortune helps those daring.*

CHAPTER 9
BREAKING AND ENTERING

President Holzer called the towering figure standing at the threshold of his office. "Come in and close the door. We have a problem."

Chief Glenburn walked in, ignoring the chair and waiting for his marching orders.

Charles' approach was direct and to the point. "Dr. Wilson's secretary has stolen research papers from the school. She is refusing to hand over the files. No doubt to retaliate for her boss' dismissal," he began. "Look for a summer trip to Italy he took five years ago. These documents are essential to support our academic claims and secure the award. This disgruntled employee is jeopardizing the good standing of this school."

Chief Glenburn stood at attention absorbing every word and nuances. He had the smug smile of a hired sword plastered over his face. Tall and wiry, with a fuzz of white hair cropped short, he nodded. His steely blue eyes looked at the window giving onto the parking lot. He searched and found the secretary's car. His plain clothes and unmarked Crown Vic were perfect today. He confirmed that his mark was at work. Good. She had the grad student with her.

The chief drove twice around the block casing the neighborhood, knowing that most residents were working. Lily Lane was an old street lined with gentrified dwellings purchased by people from off. At the last count, two doctors, a lawyer and three bankers lived there in pristine remodeled houses.

He remembered Lily Lane from his childhood. The homes lining the street had once belonged to generations of city founders. Back when he was a boy, they had gleamed with fresh coats of paint. Cast-iron benches, rocking chairs and wicker sofas invited conversations. White columns braced the wraparound porches, graced with potted ferns and urns. The chief longed for a simpler time.

The few strongholds remaining shook off decades of layered paint. Northerners had long ago purchased entire blocks of Victorian residences along the peninsula. Feuding family members, entangled in heirs' disputes no one won, let their homes go to seed. Absentee property owners subdivided mansions into apartments, but for the most part, gentrification was inevitable.

Miss Bunnie came from a long line of pharmacists and druggists. Her father and brothers ran the Lily Pharmacy & General Store for the better part of his youth. His fondest childhood memories included buffing off the bottom of his shorts at the deli counter. He loved to sit and swivel on the bar stool with his best friend Peter. Albert Dupree, Miss Bunnie's brother, had run the place with a firm but fair hand. Chief Glenburn still remembered the disappointed look he gave him on a hot summer day, when to ward off boredom he had stolen a few candies. Mr. Dupree caught him but did not call his parents; instead he offered him a job. It was the end of his life of crime and the launch of a summer job making root beer floats for local kids.

Guilt crept in Chief Glenburn's mind–a disquieting emotion for a typically unburdened man. He had committed a long list of white-collar infractions for Watson over the years, but he had never felt the slight twinge of shame. His mission was plain: protect Watson from those who could harm it. This was different.

He could never repay the president for taking a chance on him. His brush with the Roanoke Police Department's disciplinary board left him dazed and hurt. Local departments had banned him. Even large box companies were hesitant. He could not even rent himself as a cop anywhere. He applied for the position at Watson, never expecting to be hired. During the interview, President Holzer quizzed him on his various skills and, satisfied, offered him a job.

Chief Glenburn had been sober for the past fifteen years. He had pledged himself to the school and its president. His duty was to protect the university and keep law and order within its walls. He rationalized his abuse of power as a necessary step to promote the general good of Watson. He hid students' follies, deleted files and expunged records when needed.

President Holzer always clothed his requests in the cloak of plausible deniability and gave him free range of the school. They both operated in a nebulous world of innuendos, allusions and veiled suggestions. The chief had become an expert at reading his superior's thoughts and moods, but this order was different and left him wondering.

Miss Bunnie was an institution at Watson and in the neighborhood. He knew that she was loyal to Dr. Wilson, but he could not picture this genteel woman stealing anything. Her life story was common knowledge in the neighborhood. She had married late, never had children, and lost her husband in the prime of his life. She had faced personal tragedy with grace and a stubborn streak admired by all.

Chief Glenburn parked a few blocks away from Lily Lane and approached the house on foot. He spotted the telltale wisteria bush and walked to the back of the home.

Miss Bunnie's house stood on a two-acre lot, a rarity in the neighborhood. It backed Mrs. Manigault's overgrown and dilapidated land. The spunky black woman was always home except on Sundays when she wore her white suit and large plumed hat to church. She would report his visit to her neighbor if he was not prudent. The chief was careful but not overly concerned. The old woman's vision had declined over the years but her hearing was still razor-sharp.

He was progressing past a small shed when a shriek stopped him in his track. He looked down and saw a mess of ruffled feathers. He had stepped over two nesting hens in the bushes and crushed their eggs. The clucking was so strident it alarmed and raised Mrs. Manigault to the rescue. She stood at the threshold of her kitchen door a can of dried mealworms in hand. A frantic look on her face, looking to the sky for a chicken hawk, she called her free ranging fowls inside the coop. "Come in girls! Hurry!"

Chief Glenburn ducked in the mess of splattered egg and dove into a prickly pear cactus. He broke his fall with his left arm and felt barbs imbed in his leather jacket. His bare hand was not so lucky and landed in a mass of purplish fruits. The pain was instantaneous. He jumped up as if licked by flames. Fleshy green pads stuck to his coat held by vicious long spines. Barbed tiny hair like bristles brushed against his left hand leaving a swath of fire. He hurried toward the back porch cursing the infernal creatures. Everyone was keeping fowls these days. *Damn chicken!*

Despite his setback, the chief reached the home in seconds. He took out a tension wrench, ran a small pick along the pins, sliding back and forth with his workable hand. The door opened with ease. He was in the mudroom before anyone noticed. A blast of cold air greeted him. An ancient cooling unit kept the air flowing in the house, a set of lungs breathing oxygen into the home. The wooden floor creaked, and the parquet echoed his every move.

He had always wondered what the inside of this historical home looked like, and he now had his answer. Despite its evident decline, the house displaced an impressive pedigree. The tall wood panels smelled of polish, lemon and wax. Doors lifted their intricate carvings toward high ceilings. Whoever had decorated this house had done it with love and devotion. The view from the wraparound porch awed him with its loveliness. A brick-lined path slopped towards the ocean, past a lush vegetable garden and a chicken coop. The afternoon light cast a serene glow on the waterway. A sea breeze ran its fingers through the marsh, sending ripples among the Sweetgrass. The radiance of the South, encapsulated in this vista, brought him to tears. He marveled at the southern grit that Miss Bunnie displayed in the face of adversity. She was still holding on to this prime real estate property on her modest salary. He guessed that every penny helped stem the tide of decay. The repairs alone could engulf any budget. His hand pulsated with pain and his heart felt shame at this incursion.

He picked the lock and gained access within seconds. Impatient to complete his assignment, Chief Glenburn entered a quaint room. He felt the ludicrous tone of this mission turn into a mockery. He was invading a respectable southern woman's boudoir, ruffling through petticoats, looking for a mysterious file.

The chief stopped and glimpsed at ancient pictures of the Lily Lane pharmacy and its proud owners. A small child with curls, surrounded by a serious looking man and four teenage boys, posed next to the matriarch. They looked stern expect for the young girl flashing a dazzling smile. Miss Bunnie had aged beyond recognition, but the grin remained intact, he noted. *This is a wild goose chase.*

He rummaged through the powder room and the kitchen. Copper pots and pans dangled from forged iron racks, suspended from the ceiling by sturdy metal chains. An herb garden, overgrown by aromatic rosemary, grew in the windowsill. On the wall, an incongruous ceramic tile with the words *Bella Vita* hung over a braid of dusty garlic bulbs. A large butcher-block table stood in the center. In the middle, a curved indentation witnessed the many meals prepared by generations of Dupree women.

He felt a pang of sadness at her depleted family tree. Miss Bunnie had lost all her brothers to the Vietnam

War. Taken early, they left no legacy; no children to help her weather the storm of old age. Anger flared within Chief Glenburn. This mission was testing him. Miss Bunnie represented his history, his tradition. *How could she be a suspect?* She was a stronghold of civility and a relic of ages past, a time capsule of sorts. He was going through her knickers, like a pervert.

After two decades living in the South, President Holzer could not relate to the *beenyahs.* He was a *comeyah* and by definition oblivious to southern subtleties.

The chief walked through the formal dining room. He could picture Mrs. Dupree holding court on holidays, receiving relatives during the summer. This space had marked milestones until the demise of Bunnie's generation. Brothers did not return from the war. Grandchildren did not grace the home and playful voices did not warm a heart.

Distracted by poignant memories, Chief Glenburn walked into the living room and stumbled on a pile of folders spilling out of a storage box. He grabbed the wall, cursed and looked around, stunned.

He was standing in the middle of a sea of paper. Cardboard boxes littered the floor. Most were open, a few closed. The folders bore the familiar Watson logo, emblazoned in garnet and gold. He counted twelve containers. They displayed names of French artists and their corresponding eras, all labeled with dates and locations.

He followed a path, leading from one of the overstuffed chairs to the sofa. How could she have taken all this? How did the president guess? *How did I miss it?* He had been there when Dr. Wilson bagged his personal affair, and he sure had not packed twelve larges boxes. He flared in anger at the deception. He knew that he faced an extended search and little time to complete it.

Chief Glenburn took reference photographs of the room with his cell phone. His instructions were to retrieve the specific files and leave no trace of his passage. He gave a cursory glance at the containers, but he only saw French names. He examined the storage boxes, searched the folders and the elusive Florence data. Folders yielded to his search without success. He tried to put everything back in its place, but doubted they could notice his passage in this mess.

He found a smaller box next to the sofa, closed and labeled Firenze, Italia, 2010. *This is it!* With precious little time to waste, and his left hand wounded, he riffled through the folder. The chief had never known the president to exhibit such obsessive behavior. His curiosity peaked, he planned to solve the mystery and gain advantage on his boss.

He looked at his watch and felt time slip away. He had less than forty-eight hours, but more than enough time to complete the task. *The documents should be there.* The folders, indexed and alphabetized, appeared in order but one was missing. He looked the sides of the chair, underneath and under the cushions to no avail. Someone else had the file.

The Kegan graduate student and Dr. Caldwell were his two prime suspects. The folder was upstairs in her room or in the professor's office or house. This complication was just a temporary setback. He started for the stairs when he heard the key turn in the front door lock and people come in. He listened to voices coming from the kitchen and disappeared in the dark mudroom.

"I think we're getting close," he heard Miss Bunnie say. "We've connected the mystery to Florence, but we're still missing the big picture. Let's go through the box again tonight after supper."

"Where is the wand? I can scan while you search," the man said.

The chief slipped out of the house deeply troubled by the latest turn of event. Scanned and digitized, the documents could no longer be contained. *It may be too late.*

CHAPTER 10
BLUE EGGSHELLS

Sophie looked at the folders with suspicion. She was a stickler for organized chaos and noticed subtle and minute change to her environment. Something was not right. Two boxes had been moved, the tops opened, and several folders taken out. She was meticulous and did not leave her space in such disarray. No one had access to the research besides the four of them.

"Someone's been there," Sophie said. They turned in unison to face her.

"Who?" Bunnie asked. "I recalled locking the house and nothing looks disturbed."

"The papers are displaced. Look at this," she said, picking up a manila folder. "There is eggshell, yolk and grass on several of the files."

"Egg yolk?" they repeated.

"Did we cook with eggs today?" Sophie asked. Bunnie nodded in the negative. They walked to the mudroom and inspected the deadbolt. It was unlatched.

"I may have forgotten to latch it," Bunnie ventured, doubting her own statement.

Sophie led the way and stepped out in the garden. "Let's look in the yard."

"You three look in the back. I'm going to chat with Marnee," Bunnie said and stepped out of the kitchen.

They walked past Rosalie's pen, toward Mrs. Manigault's shed, and stumbled effortlessly on the crime scene. A dozen eggs lay trampled in the underbrush, along with a flattened cactus.

"A chicken hawk, may be?" David asked.

"No, they pluck them off the ground, they don't trample them to death," Sophie noted. "It looks as if someone walked right into their roosting nest and trashed the eggs. Look, the tracks lead to our house. The egg yolk is still wet."

Bunnie rejoined her friends and reported on her conversation with her neighbor. "Mrs. Manigault had a fright this afternoon. She heard a racket outside, less than an hour ago, and called her hens inside. She thought a chicken hawk attacked her hens. Her eyesight is very poor, but I know better. The evidence points to him," she added, channeling her best imitation of Agatha Christie.

They all turned to Bunnie, understanding her meaning; but remaining silent, afraid to cross that bridge.

"It's the only thing that makes sense," Sophie agreed "No one else we know is after these files, only him. But I don't see him breaking and entering."

"Not *him*," Bunnie explained. "His June-bug."

"You mean they've bugged the place?" Marie asked.

"Bugged?" Bunnie asked, turning her mystified face towards her friends. "His *June-bug*. President Holzer is the duck and the chief is the June-bug."

"The chief had motive and opportunity. He has done other unsavory things for his boss over the years. He has hushed scandals, provided alibis, erased documents, if the gossip is true. Such behavior gets noticed and flagged unless you have someone's protection," Marie admitted, trying to keep her friend's imagination in check, and not doing a good job.

"Dr. Wilson either knew too much or had something President Holzer coveted. He probably believes we have it. He will stop at nothing to retrieve it, including breaking and entering. This is becoming a dangerous hunt," concluded Bunnie.

"A hunt?"

"Yes," she added with a smug smile. "A treasure hunt!"

"What for?" asked David.

"Art, of course. What else?" she added, her mind racing well ahead of her friends. "President Holzer is a visual arts aficionado. I don't see him bothering with anything else."

Marie knew that they were jumping to conclusions but it made odd sense to her. "Isn't everything catalogued in the museum?"

"Yes, in the new building. The older buildings still hold pieces we have not inventoried. The president has always brushed aside our requests for automation," answered Bunnie.

"Then, it's in that box. The Florence files," Sophie pointed to the sofa.

"Bunnie, what did you bring back from Italy that summer?" Marie probed.

"We brought several crates back to the U.S. The Italian authorities zealously documented and inspected our purchases. I don't think they'd let us bring the David back home," Bunnie winked.

"It can't be the Maiolica potteries. They are in the museum. The marble sculptures were small sculptures purchased from a surrounding farm near Carrara. I have not seen them since the trip. We have so many artifacts in storage. They must still be in Franklin's basement," she added.

"Dr. Wilson did not bring paintings back from Italy?" Marie asked.

"No, he only brought back potteries and sculptures."

"We know where the potteries are. We need to find the sculptures," Sophie urged.

They grilled chicken and corn on the cob, sitting on the porch with the Florence box. David read the titles of the folders. Marie scanned the files and emailed them to Sophie who uploaded them online. Together, they spent well into the night creating a digital record of their findings, while Isabelle slept upstairs with Dood.

"The computer program will find the associations, references and connections we are missing," said Marie.

On cue, a litany of great names popped up on the screen. "Mino da Fiesole, Desiderio da Settignano and Benedetto de Maiano," read Sophie. "This is a 'Who's Who' of the Golden Age of Italian sculpture. We might as well copy and paste an art history book."

"Florence was at the heart of the High Renaissance," Marie explained. "Botticelli, Michelangelo, and Leonardo da Vinci created in this magnificent city. Bertoldo, Savoranola, Lorenzo Il Magnifico lived here. The Bonfire of Vanities took place on its main square. These artists and princes contributed to this incredible flight of humanism. We are searching for a treasure in one of the most studied and recorded periods in history. I doubt we'll find anything of importance."

Marie picked up a pile of folders and set it aside on the coffee table.

"My mentor always said nothing was new in Renaissance Florence. Michelangelo was a prolific writer. He left a treasure trove of correspondence during an eighty nine-year old lifespan. Da Vinci documented everything. Scholars have studied these giants with sharpened quills for centuries. There is nothing else to find."

Bunnie stood up, a folder in hand. "The sculptures are significant; I can sense it. We need to find them. The hurricane preparations will distract the president."

"We need to prepare as well," David warned. "The hurricane is veering north and we should get ready to leave shortly."

Earlier in the morning, Bunnie had surprised her friends by agreeing to leave when Hanna became a Cat 5. The storm was now threatening the entire East Coast. Mrs. Manigault's extended family forcibly evacuated her a few hours ago.

The hurricane had torn apart the Caribbean Islands leaving a path of complete destruction in its wake. Television channels broadcast the monster with manic precision. Marie was grateful for David's pragmatic behavior and Bunnie's calm demeanor. They kept her anxiety in check.

She thought of her house, still packed in boxes. Her downsizing was continuing. She shook her head at the prospect of distilling the essence of her life to a few suitcases. The exercise was freeing and somewhat comical. Marie had stored her mother's oil paintings by the front door. In a box, she packed her grandfather's love letters and poems to her grandmother. She had packed her grandparents' Tunisian memorabilia by the entrance door. A pink container held Isabelle's favorite stuffed animals and school keepsakes. Marie planned to feed her soul if not her body. She knew that her choices were emotional, sentimental and impractical. She could replace everything else. How did you distill the essence of your life in a suitcase? She had wrestled with that question all morning. In her choices, she was letting go of the past and of the crushing weight that threatened to engulf her.

David, who was better at planning emergency road trips than debating Renaissance Italy, sprung to action and led their evacuation. He had prepared an emergency kit for each of his friends. He felt a visceral need to keep these women out of harm's way. They had fallen to the lure of a treasure hunt in the midst of the greatest hurricane in recent history. He planned to keep them safe during their quest. His purpose was ordinary, but he was fine with that. He knew something was amiss and remained on guard. He agreed that the president was behind the sordid plot and suggested calling the police. Bunnie refused.

"And say what?" she asked. "The chief broke into my house and rummaged through my knickers? I feel so violated, and that stirs my stew!"

Calling the authorities, they agreed, could not solve their dilemma but instead expose their misdeeds and focus the police investigation in the wrong direction. Why call more attention on their activities? The episode upset David more than he led on. He insisted they spend the night at Bunnie's house. He planned to sleep on the sofa with the files while Marie and Isabelle would take a room upstairs.

"We need to complete preparations for the hurricane," he added. "I'll finish boarding the windows downstairs while you keep on scanning the files. We will each carry our evacuation kits, food and water. I've made arrangements for us to stay at my cousin's home in the mountains."

"We need to find the file before Hanna gets here," Sophie reminded them.

"And I need to get a change of clothes for us if we are to sleep at Bunnie's tonight," Marie replied.

"I'll go with you," said David. Isabelle, nestled on the sofa, slept her excitement away and did not notice them leave.

They walked the short trip in silence enjoying the cooler evening temperatures, the sound of the tree frogs and the smell of the pluff mud.

"I love it," said Marie.

"Pluff mud? Yes, you either love it or hate it. I know I'm home when I smell it," said David enjoying the mélange of decay and saltwater floating in the air.

David saw a one-story brick house with a white picket fence and a tree house perched on a towering live oak. He knew they had arrived. Looking for signs of forced entry, he walked ahead and blocked Marie's path. The house looked peaceful and undisturbed. She watched him open the door with the key she had given him. He entered the premises and was back outside in an instant. "Come on in. Everything looks fine."

Marie watched him, feeling centered and calm. She trusted him. Her arrival in the South amidst hurricanes, toxic bosses and thievery left her dumbfounded. She had expected her familiar walls to rise up and her alarms to ring a quick retreat. Instead, she was more resilient than she had been in years. Her new friends empowered her to dare and hope. They carried individual fragilities, which when coming together became strengths. Together, they grew stronger that the sum of their parts.

"Do you see anything missing or displaced?" David asked.

Marie went through her files and the authentication dossier awaiting her signature. "Everything is in order. As you can see I have not unpacked yet," she grinned, walking past a wall of unpacked boxes.

"We maybe overreacting with the eggshell bandit," David answered. "There might be a normal explanation."

"You're right. Much to do about nothing," Marie said, picking up a change of clothes for her daughter and herself. "Let's go back to Bunnie's house. She hasn't decided yet what she's taking with her."

Marie reached for her keys and heard a light crunch. She looked at the wooden floor, bent down and retrieved a piece of blue eggshell.

CHAPTER 11
THE SOUTH IS BURNING

"The file wasn't there," Chief Glenburn admitted, still surprised at his failure.

"That's impossible!" President Holzer answered, his voice rising in anger.

"I spent two hours at Miss Bunnie's house and one hour at Dr. Caldwell's place."

Charles felt his irritation rise, choking his thoughts and belaboring his breathing. He had kept a strong hold on the school for two decades. He moved his chess pieces with care, always in control, never losing a game, until now.

"Get the damn papers. No more excuses." Charles snapped at the chief.

This past week had unraveled in splendid chaos. John's secretary commandeered files that belonged to the school. She had questioned his authority and searched for blueprints of the old buildings. The chief's briefing further unsettled him. They had connected Florence to the marble sculptures! They had covered more ground in a month than he had in years. His departure for Italy was fast approaching and the move of his collection was in the final stages of preparation. To lose it now was insufferable.

"You are positive you saw the box?"

"Yes, the box was there and most of the files, except for the documents you requested."

"Are you sure that the piano tuner was there?" Charles, who could not see the relation between these four, now considered them adversaries. He was loath to cast a wider net and risk involving more people. *Victori spolia,* to the victor the spoil. He must decisive and show no mercy.

"Return to Dupree's house and find the papers," he ordered. "These old mansions are accidents waiting to happen. They have faulty wiring and crumbling structures. I wouldn't be surprised if that shack burned to the ground sooner than later."

Chief Glenburn looked up at the president searching for clarification. *He is asking me to commit arson?* The president had already moved to another project and dismissed him. The chief realized he had just walked into a trap. A fluttering insect caught in a large web, he knew that every protest, every fearful breath, could bring the predator closer. He had graduated from a life of petty crime, to arson and now attempted murder. The orders were transparent. He was to burn the place.

His standing at the school and his career were at risk. A possible stint in prison for a long list of past transgressions was not far. President Holzer, he guessed, had documented each of his indiscretions. He should have known better than to stand in the path of his wrath. He had observed President Holzer's modus operandi over two decades; yet, he had nothing tangible against him. The president gave no specific orders, left no phone recordings or paper trails that could lead back to him. No proof of wrongdoings pointed to the president of the famous school.

A Northerner had just asked a Southerner to torch the South.

This madness had to stop. He had been blind too long. He had to take his life back. The chief planned to turn the table on this carpetbagger and run him out of town. The problem of Bunnie Dupree remained. He had to make good on his orders before turning the tide on Holzer. He will never meet him again without a wire. Two could play that game, and he had enough training to build a case.

It was ten o'clock in the evening by the time Chief Glenburn returned to Miss Bunnie's house. His mind was bursting with questions. *Why is this file so important?* Whatever it was, the president was intent on securing it, no matter the cost. Torching a building at night, with occupants inside *was* attempted murder. It was a desperate step for a distressed mind. He planned to solve the mystery after the hurricane. For now, he needed to convince Charles he was still his pawn.

The chief drove to Rebecca Lane and parked outside Piggy Wiggly unconcerned. He knew the security cameras were fakes, unable to record his visit. He walked through several backyards to avoid Mrs. Manigault's chickens and approached the back of the house unnoticed. He located a spot to start the fire with the chemicals he transported in his bag. The chief planned to continue the pretense. He wanted enough dirt on President Holzer to shake the status quo and make going to the police impossible for either one of them. He was running out of time. He'd heard him talk of his approaching retirement and couldn't let him leave with a briefcase full of incriminating evidence.

Back on Lily Lane, the chief watched the house from afar, noting the camaraderie uniting friends. Gathered around a stack of documents, he witnessed their animated discussion. The fullness of lives engaged in a common purpose made him question his orders. *What was worth threatening life and property?*

The answer to the mystery was in that house. He needed to protect it to solve the riddle. He sprayed the accelerant inside the woodshed, threw a match and closed the door. Within seconds, voracious flames licked the small building, hungry for wood. Greater destruction, he could not let happen. He grabbed a disposable phone and dialed a number. The phone rang eight times before a disoriented voice answered. The chief let out a guttural "Fire!" into the receiver. He heard a commotion in the kitchen and saw Mrs. Manigault emerge in her slippers and housedress.

"Oh my!" she yelled, watching her neighbor's shed engulfed in flames. She marched towards Bunnie's home shouting, "Fire, fire!" She met Sophie outside speaking to the 9-1-1 operator, a white dog barking at her heels. The chief felt guilty for involving the frail neighbor in his plot, but it was the price to pay to save the main residence.

He retreated further in the shadows. The scene mesmerized him. The grad student was still on the phone, poised and calm. She answered questions and provided information. The piano tuner had turned on the outside faucet and was spraying the walls of the main structure with water. *Smart.* The shed could not be saved, but he directed his energy to saving the main house. The chief saw him win that fight. Distant sirens were fast approaching, bringing reinforcement.

Dr. Caldwell attended to the needs of the secretary and her neighbor. She sat them on Mrs. Manigault's porch, away from the fire. Clucking and bleating in panic, the animals had sought refuge in the neighbor's yard. At her side was a young girl carrying a small dog. Both mother and daughter were soothing their charges as help arrived. Half a dozen neighbors fought the fire with pails of water. The sirens let out strident calls and the fire trucks illuminated the dark skies. In a flurry of activities, he saw the local fire department spring to action. They hooked up to a fire hydrant, deployed the hoses and extinguished the fire in minutes.

The chief looked at the four friends and felt their determination, cohesion and unity. He also spotted a beige folder clenched under the grad student's arm. He was on the right track. People turned to their most valuable possessions in an emergency. In the midst of pandemonium, the young woman had retrieved and saved one thing. That file contained the key to the mystery.

CHAPTER 12
BLOOD DIAMOND

They watched the embers of the smoking shed well into the night, sitting on plastic lawn chairs. Isabelle rested comfortably in her mother's arms. In the early hours of dawn, they convened around the kitchen table. Marie laid her daughter on the sofa where Dood soon joined her.

Sophie watched the shed reduced to ashes and thought of sacrifices, large and small, exacted from those she loved. She thought of her own inner struggles to create art and paint her life story. She credited Petra with igniting her new artistic path. Obsessed with giving flight to the images swirling in her mind, she had not stopped painting since her return from Jordan. Restless and exhausted, she kept on painting. Her parents grew concerned, having hoped for a smoother transition for their daughter. Her fire grew inward. Subtle for the untrained eye, the change wreaked havoc on their peace of mind. The gentle child was still there– seeking love and understanding. The woman within balked at any advice and guidance. The kindness of childhood had given way to the steeliness of adulthood. It was as if the sands of the *Wadi Rum* had desiccated the tenderness of youth into a striated inscrutable sphinx.

Alone in her studio, nursing the pain of change she had inflicted on everyone around her, Sophie completed a collection of sand and fire. The impact of the scents, colors and the blend of history, architecture and human commerce led her to create an acclaimed solo art show in Boston. That extraordinary success landed her the prestigious artist-in-residence position at the famed Watson School of the Arts. She jumped at the first opportunity to leave Boston and explore new shores.

Her arrival in the south had given birth to new inspiration and influences. Sophie kept on painting. Given the body of work she had created since moving to the land of pluff mud and immutable oaks, she was ready for her winter solo show in Atlanta.

The painting rhythm she had maintained since first arriving on the Carolina coast came to an abrupt halt with Hanna. The storm had unhinged her. The bulk of her pieces were too large to transport in her car and she had stored them in the new student center. Hurricane Hanna's cone of probability loomed so wide that there was nowhere to hide. She prayed her work would survive the storm.

Sophie climbed the steps to the porch, carrying eggs from the coop, tomatoes and basil from the garden. She opened the door and interrupted an animated discussion punctuated by a barrage of questions from Bunnie.

"How far could you go for art? Would you steal? Kill?"

"It depends on the piece of art," laughed Marie as she grabbed a mixing bowl and started whisking the eggs. "Are you asking if President Holzer could steal?"

"Back to the blue eggshell topic?" Sophie asked, walking in the room.

"We know that the president would steal, but to accuse him of attempted murder is quite another matter," Marie continued.

"Art history is littered with the blood of thieves and usurpers," Bunnie countered. "I was at the Smithsonian years ago and saw the Hope Diamond. It reminded of what people can do for forty-five carats of brilliance."

"I saw it once," David said, eager to join in on a topic he finally knew. "The blue diamond was found in India in the seventeenth century. A French merchant sold it to the Sun King for cash and a title. It was recut and passed on to other French and English kings. A rich London banker named Hope gave it a name. The Hope Diamond came to America in the early 1900s and was even sent through regular mail. Diamond merchant Harry Winston donated it to the National Museum of

Natural History to set up a national gem collection. It is now at the Smithsonian, insured for $250 million."

"And don't forget the curse," Bunnie added, always the sleuth. "The Hope Diamond is linked to suicide, murder, torture, disgrace, abandonment, bankruptcy and quartering."

"Curses and superstitions have always surrounded art, particularly during the Victorian era," Marie said. "The curse of the Hope Diamond was no different. It added mystique to the piece of art and increased its value. I must admit it was a great marketing ploy."

"Take Van Gogh, for example," Sophie said. "Scientists have just now uncovered a connection between the idea of mathematical turbulences and the movement in his *Starry Night.*"

"They proved that in his psychotic state, Van Gogh captured one of science's most elusive theories–that of turbulent flow and fluid dynamics," she added.

"The most I could make out of this unsolved mathematical riddle is that turbulence flow is self-similar and produces an energy cascade. The stars and moon you see swirling in the famous painting depict this phenomenon."

"Impressionists achieved luminance, but turbulence was particular to Van Gogh's psychotic state. He did not achieve turbulence in his calmer state. Imagine how much more special this painting is now. It illustrates Van Gogh's ability, in his darkest time, to capture one of nature's most baffling physics notion–one hundred years before scientists began studying it."

"I'm not sure I believe in the idea that artists must experience suffering to create great art. But I believe that investors and critics demand suffering in art," Marie interjected.

"Most art investors are peeping Toms," Sophie said. "They feed on the agony of artists. They will not consider a piece of art worthy if it has not been forged in a maelstrom of pain, struggle and conflict. To make the piece unique, the artist must be sacrificed at the altar of art–an ear, sanity, or worse. Pain enhances its value, makes it more marketable. A collector always seeks its pint of blood. They envy those who create; maybe their impotence is offset by the suffering of others."

"Owning a piece of history, of bloody history, transforms you. Some people, captivated by the agony of man and the exalted art they produce, become obsessed with collecting such art," Marie agreed. "To answer your question, I believe that President Holzer could steal to secure a priceless piece of art. Could he kill for it? Yes, I suppose he could, if he felt threatened with the loss of it. It could be the next logical step for an obsessed mind."

"I hope we won't find out," David said.

CHAPTER 13
THE HUNTED

"I am surprised that the shed was the only building lost," Charles snapped, his temper rising.

"The next-door neighbor alerted the occupants of the house," Chief Glenburn answered. He avoided naming persons and places. He wanted to stay as neutral as possible in the illegal recording he was making of his boss.

Charles was mystified. How incompetent was the chief? Was he becoming a liability? Charles was losing control of his employees with each passing day–days he couldn't afford to waste.

"No news on the Florence files?"

"Not yet," the chief answered.

The chief was guttural. Charles had developed a keen sense of the suspicious and the extraordinary. He was an expert at reading people. *What's with him?* His employee so placid and amiable had become cryptic and useless. *He knows something.*

Dr. Caldwell and company were becoming a threat, but he had expected Chief Glenburn to stay loyal. He was now fighting on two fronts.

"What would you want me to do next?" he asked.

"I pay you to think and act," Charles snapped. "Why are you asking me?"

"I need to be clear on what you want."

Charles was in full alert mode. The chief had never known failure while working for him all these years. Two failures in a week were unprecedented. He reviewed scenarios that could have led to his entrapment, and could not find one. Why was the chief so suspicious? He did not know of his collection; Charles was certain of it. The president had not relied on him to install his security alert and always met with him at the office.

On special occasions, he opened the downstairs of his home to guests and board members, but he always kept his private collection out of sight. A passionate lover did not share his passion with anyone. He had come close once but had resisted the urge to impress a love interest. Charles raked his brain and could not find an error. He was always home for maintenance and never contracted within the county for repair and maintenance.

Charles had taken extraordinary measures to protect his collection. And yet, despite his efforts, Dr. Caldwell had begun to unveil his secret. His hubris, he admitted, was to believe his control over the chief was total. He had miscalculated and tipped him off with his obsessive behavior. His wish to leave this oppressive and parochial South superseded all. Nothing mattered anymore but his upcoming move to Florence.

The president realized the scales still leaned in his favor. He had documented Chief Glenburn's excesses from the start. His subordinate was trying to incriminate him and he needed to restore his supremacy before he lost control. He looked at his head of security and dismissed him.

"The hurricane is coming. Get on it," he snarled.

Chief Glenburn left the President's Office feeling dejected. He had somehow managed to show his hand and alert his opponent of his own suspicions. He had to shake him off or forever watch his back. *I must get in his house and find the clue.*

The chief planned to use the impending storm as a cover for his investigation. He had to seize the opportunity and pay the president's home a visit. His knowledge of art history was a joke, but that did not bother him. He looked at the president's schedule and confirmed his attendance at two meetings. Free to spy on his boss, he reached the president's home in minutes.

The imposing mansion, surrounded by Spanish moss-draped oaks, offered him privacy. The towering evergreen trees spread out their trunk-sized limbs across the lawn. They preceded the incorporation of Watson. He believed they would outlive the institution. *The South will prevail.*

The American colonial house focused the attention on the large front portico. Chief Glenburn, who preferred a more discreet approach, broke in through a side door. He disabled the school security and gained access in seconds. He had been in the house several times before, but never past the Great Hall. His boss had resisted stepping up security, pointing to the town's non-existing crime rate.

The rebuff from the president had been swift. "Our record speaks for itself, and I refuse to feed this existential anxiety. I have enough security for this place."

Chief Glenburn was now glad for the minimal security. He came in through the back of the raised English basement used for storage and maintenance. He climbed up the service stairway and reached the Great Hall.

Designed to awe visitors, this place always underwhelmed him. It was too ornate for his taste. The engravings were too flowery, the moldings an endless race of daffodils and dogwood. The tan color of the wall panels was bland and devoid of personality. It was the polar opposite to his place by the lake adorned with hunting trophies. President Holzer lived in a museum, a fact that would drive the chief mad. The immaculate home was of course on the National Register of Historic Places.

Chief Glenburn swept the public areas and did not find a clue. He continued through the Withdrawal Room, a list in hand, cross-referencing the art on loan at the president's house. The art was there, on display. Nothing was missing; all pieces accounted for and showcased in public spaces.

The chief opened the doors to the library. Books on the Italian Renaissance littered a large table. An imposing mahogany desk displayed gilded papers and old maps. His library tour concluded, he climbed the Stair Hall. Carved lotus and squash blossoms ran along the wainscot, banister and brackets. The grandeur of the place was oppressive. He looked around holding onto the mahogany railing and began his ascent to the Upper Great Hall.

The chief glanced at his blueprints to get his bearing. They dated back to the early 1920s, and showed a suite of rooms occupying the entire second floor with a long hallway traversing the home. He expected to find the place untouched since renovations to this house would necessitate nothing less than an act of Congress. He continued up the stairs, looking at his map and peaked through the second floor banister. What he saw stopped him in his track.

CHAPTER 14
THE DEEP WEB

Chief Glenburn sealed his fate with every step he took inside the president's home. The mercy that Charles might have shown him after twenty years of faithful service evaporated in a burst of rage. Charles looked at the small screen and saw his home breached by someone he knew and trusted. That fact alone shattered the universe he had constructed. Subordinates should know their position and keep their station. The chief had upset the status quo at his own peril.

Charles' home was under surveillance and monitored from a remote device. A New York City firm specializing in high-end security systems had installed the unit. The president's home, while appearing easy to breach, was impregnable. His collection was secure. Chief Glenburn's unfocused search, far from reassuring and appeasing Charles, infuriated him. Even bumbling fools can make connections and uncover secrets, he thought.

Every touch, every glance, and every breath taken in his home was going to cost the chief everything. Charles knew that his *sanctum sanctorum* was unreachable, but his pride had taken a blow.

The president never forgot or forgave. He was an encyclopedia of wrongs paid and retributions exacted. He filed them away in his mind and waited for the suitable moment to exact revenge. His sense of time was elastic and fluid. He sprung traps on unsuspecting offenders long after transgressions occurred.

He refrained from rushing home to catch the thief in the act. Instead, he continued to witness the breach of his home. The chief never stopped by his table near the window. He concentrated instead on his High Renaissance period desk. On the worktable laid books and clues pointing to his secret. The chief was on the right track and something was afoot, but he remained obtuse to the real treasure. His presence in his home dispelled any notion they could still work together. The chief had to go.

What an ingrate! After all I've done for him! I gave him his life back after his Roanoke fiasco.

The line between law enforcement and thievery was a tenuous one, he thought. Temptation, in its myriad of forms, always got the best of most. Charles did not have this conundrum. Individuals of greater intellect ignored petty laws.

He had inherited from his father's long tenure in the Senate a list of contacts recorded with a meticulous handwriting in a black leather journal. The book contained names of talented individuals operating on the fringe of society. These contacts, vetted over the years, could for the right price offer unique services.

Charles selected the name of someone he had used before. Bob was a single, middle-aged man, with an elaborate flyover spread across his mottled skull. They met once in New York City to establish trade. Bob was a diminutive rodent with a penchant for dark places. He had a gift for navigating the far reaches of the Deep Web unmolested.

Charles had never shared with the chief any of his private contacts. They both lived into two separate worlds, never destined to connect. The chief was a sluggish old catfish swimming in a tannin-ridden swamp. Charles was a sleek shark coursing through the wide ocean. The chief wanted to start an unsanctioned life of crime? Charles would be happy to oblige. Bob could reconstruct, for the right price, a new digital footprint for his mark. The violation of his home signaled the chief's descent into the nine circles of Hell.

"I want him destroyed," Charles spoke into a disposable cell phone. "No pension, reputation, or savings left. No friends or family to rescue him. Build him a new identity. Make the children small and the offenses specific and heinous and send the data to the FBI. He must become a pariah to everyone and to himself."

Charles marveled at the ease with which he kept his ventures private in the Deep Web. The scale of what laid underneath the surface astonished him. It was the tip of the iceberg, where invisible sites hid their content in dark places. For a large sum of money, Bob had inducted Charles into the Dark Web, a part of the Deep Web even more shadowy–a crime-ridden cesspool. He taught him to access sites that catered to his interests.

Charles found it amusing that the Dark Web, now rife with illegal trade, had first been a government program. The U.S. Navy had since lost control of its tool and narrative. The underground commerce began to flourish. Human traffickers, thieves, child pornographers, assassins and a wide range of predators and exploiters now lived in the Dark Web. Charles despised its vast maze of corruption preying on the basest instincts of man. He only went there to curate his collection. He never stayed long and exited the portal once his business concluded. He exclusively dealt with an art trafficker who had purchased a dozen pieces from him through anonymous transactions.

The Deep Web was not entirely dark and toxic. A better part of it hosted the databases of libraries, universities and medical facilities. The rest housed an equal share of the hunter and the hunted. Both criminals and law enforcement agents scoured the Dark Web. Federal agents looked for illegal trade, intent on catching the next long con. Predators could, in a single sting, become prey to an elaborate security dragnet.

Charles used the Dark Web to sell his dispensable art with the encrypted procedure Bob set up for him. Within a year, Charles graduated from small illegal art sales to greater pursuits. He planned to move his core collection to Italy and sell the rest. His contacts awaited a series of final sales. Everything was set. He was ready to go and an annoying secretary would not derail him now.

CHAPTER 15
MARBLE MILK

Alone in the basement of the Franklin Building, Charles brushed his fingers along a piece of cool opalescent marble. Touching this magnificent object, he channeled the artist who had created it. He lingered on the small of the neck, the curb of the chin and the softness of the lips. For every creator rose a protector. Charles understood his role in this intelligent design. He bore witness to art and protected it. His mission was to preserve beauty, a task now threatened by the impeding storm.

To calm his heart, he touched the smooth marble and remembered Carrara. His voyage to Italy three years ago had set him on a quest that had proven nothing short of miraculous. Every step taken inside the Italian stone quarry had brought him closer to his treasure.

His epic journey began with the rental of a small camionette and Paulo, his Tuscan driver. He had hoped to enter the heart of the marbled Roman Empire in a more dignified manner, but had to settle for a rusted blue Fiat. Little more than a moped with a flatbed, the rust bucket inched up a gravel road on its way to one of the oldest marble quarries in Europe. The journey took the better part of the morning.

What first appeared as peaks encased in eternal snows were, on closer look, the exposed flank of the neighboring mountains. The Carrara quarries had existed for the past two millennia. For centuries, men had dissected the peaks in geometric patterns. Everywhere he looked, Charles saw the ruin of nature and the birth of form.

Up dizzying heights and scary switchbacks, the resolute Fiat climbed and coughed consumptive black puffs of smoke in its wake. Paulo, oblivious to the grievous sounds of his mini truck, belted out traditional Italian songs. He drove to the musical renditions of *O Sole Mio* and *Azurro.* When Paulo began singing *La Forza del Destino,* Charles prayed for safe travels. He looked at the vertiginous cliffs and saw miniature quarries and men, no bigger than ants, slicing the mountainside into large blocks.

Paulo sang and kept tempo, his amputated fingers taping on the steering wheel. Charles had observed other stonecutters in several of the villages they passed with the same physical characteristics. The maimed digits were a daily reminder of the harrowing work that permitted no mistakes. The impact of marble against soft flesh and bones was unforgiving, a brutal rite of passage for some apprentices.

Blood was part of creation. It was the price paid for creating exquisite loveliness and breathing life into stone. The equipment used to extract marble had changed with electricity and modern industry. Yet, the practice of teasing the huge blocks out of the mountainside remained unchanged. Over several days, the stonecutters inserted wedges to pry the rock from the face of the mountain. It was exacting and dangerous work.

Near the top of the mountain, the voluble opera singer pounded on his thin brakes and brought the Fiat to a screeching halt. Charles grabbed the dashboard to keep a modicum of decorum and avoid crashing through the windshield.

Paulo parked his camionette near the entrance of an underground quarry. He motioned for Charles to follow and lifted a finger to his lips. No talking at the site, he warned, one stayed focused and listened to the mountain. He showed his maimed hand; inattention could cost a man more than a few fingers. They stepped next to a large quarry pit lined with towering blocks of marble. In this bleached lunar landscape, Charles knew he had reached the heart of his obsession. Shaking him out of his trance, a truck drove by in a blizzard of white powder, dusting him in a cloud of Carrara's best.

Paulo swore volubly and led the way towards the entrance of the quarry. From his vantage point, Charles observed the ruin of nature surrounding him. Layers of the mountains peeled off and revealed geometric cuttings. The blocks glistened in the bright azure sky like bleached elephant bone yards. The sun bounced off the rough-hewn marble slabs, chasing light and shadows.

This ancient quarry predated the rise of the David or the Pieta. Classical Rome had embraced it, the Dark Ages lost it and the Renaissance had re-discovered it. Man's will in extracting luminous stones transformed drab cities into gleaming marble metropolises. Steeped in the blood and tears of generations of slaves and artisans, statuary marble invoked wealth, power and privilege. Here the mountains gave birth to sculptures and cities draped in an eternal play of light and shadows.

Charles followed Paulo into a chamber lined by soaring blocks of marble. A tall ladder, thirty feet up in the air, leaned against the side of a mammoth block. Paulo joined his coworkers for a smoke, leaving his ward behind. Charles climbed the stepladder and stood on the block to get a better view. From his vantage point, he saw the artificial light of the working lamps bounce off the blocks of marble. It played with the sound pulsating from the electric saws at work in rooms deeper within the tunnel. Galvanized by his surroundings, Charles found himself communing with the mountain better than he ever could in the cathedrals of Europe.

Paulo had explained that little had changed since Roman times. Centuries of toil had not dulled the danger inherent with his profession. Stonecutters and Renaissance sculptors, obsessed with finding flawless stones, often risked their lives seeking the perfect block.

Primal geometry enveloped Charles. He understood the mystery and the obsession buried within the mountains. Deep inside their bowels, the next David or Hercules slumbered. Golden ages came and went, fostering artistic renewal and rebirth. Inside these quarries, masterpieces awaited discovery by the giants of their age. He wished his life would have the perennial endurance of these works of art.

Charles had traveled to Italy unbeknownst to his staff and Board who believed him to be in Germany. After landing in Munich, he checked in with Watson and took occupancy of an isolated cottage. A few hours later, he boarded a train for Northern Italy, shedding his identity through several Schengen countries.

Once in Florence, he scoured libraries and local courthouses relying on his Italian to make sense of ancient papers. His quest gained momentum. Charles had found a connection in dusty records and historical archives of the famed city.

The sculptures John brought back from Tuscany were the key to a major artistic discovery. The studio where the marble odds and ends Henry found had belonged to the same family for six centuries. Charles held records attesting to the undisrupted ownership of the land. Memories and records endured in Europe. He spent the past two days connecting the sculptures to the family and to the artist. A chance connection between unrelated names had finally exposed the link.

Charles visited the marble studio where John had purchased the sculptures. The quarry and the farm had been in the same family since the early 1500s. Local artisans had been selling reproductions of well-known pieces to tourists for centuries. Many stonecutters and sculptors still lived in and around Carrara, Massa and Pietrasanta. Two millennia later, the extraction and sculpting of marble still drove the economy of an entire region. Local artisans could reproduce famous sculptures. Charles saw an artist complete in a matter of a few days a well-known piece.

Could it pass for the real thing? Charles could not believe John's luck. While seeking well-executed reproductions, he had unbeknownst to all spirited away the real thing. *Under the Carabinieri Art Squad's nose–no less.* It was now up to Charles to take the art back to Italy unnoticed. He had purchased the rest of the "odds and ends" found in the abandoned studio. The pieces, secured in a storage unit, were not far from the property he had purchased for his retirement.

Perched on his large block of marble, Charles listened to the saws cutting into the rock. He believed that the greatest call of man was to create art. He saw art everywhere, even in the depth of a quarry and in the simple process of extraction.

Religion, a famous philosopher once said, was the opium of the masses, an anesthetic to dull the brutal impact of life on a soul. Charles could not relate to man's sins, mortal or otherwise. If religion was to dull the soul, art was to exalt it. He thrived in a world stripped of accountability, free of manmade morals. He lived in a world where the divine existed in the lines of a Grecian urn or the grief of a Madonna.

The average person needed God to make sense of life and create order, subjugate and dominate. Charles instead saw God as an architect of life and form, the artist as a seer and the art as the product of that union. Far from being the judge of human frailties, God was creation and inspiration. Let the masses keep track of check and balances; Charles had a higher purpose: to protect art. He had developed for his collection the paternal feelings he had never experienced for his child. There were no laws he would not bend to protect it.

Charles noticed water dripping into a curvature within the stone. The water, mixing with airborne particles of marble dust, had created a pool of white liquid. In the depth of the quarry, Charles experienced his greatest epiphany. He dipped his fingers in the substance and felt the marble transmutes into milk. *It's all related: the discovery, the quarry, the marble,* he thought.

The stonecutters on break, Charles stepped off the ladder to explore the galleries. A few strings of electric wires, bundled and nailed to the walls, led him from one room to the other. The wet marble dust had settled on the wires and dried creating over time a shell that stuck to the wall.

Charles followed Ariadne's thread to the next gallery, to the one beyond, and suddenly looked up in awe. The sheer scale of the space, large enough to contain a cathedral, overwhelmed him. Radiant pools of milk dotted the foreign landscape, reflecting the light on their pale surface. A forest of tall columns supported the cavernous space.

Charles had arrived home after a life spent searching for the authentic. He found, in the depth of the mountains, the raw blocks that paved churches and built altars. The imagination and talent that could liberate the sculpture from its casing was nothing short of miraculous. Leaning against a pillar, Charles realized his life's journey had begun.

The ring of his cell phone jolted him from his Italian reverie and brought him back to Watson.

"Do you have it?" Charles asked, noting the chief's number.

"Yes."

"Any troubles?"

"None," the chief replied, closing the net around his boss.

CHAPTER 16

THE HIGH PLACE OF SACRIFICE

Sophie locked her studio and cast a last glance at the Intracoastal Waterway, gleaming in the distance. It always astounded her. The afternoon light was richer and sharper, but she had no time to give the view its due. They were evacuating.

She had packed up her paintings, pigments, brushes and canvases and left behind her stretchers, solvents, fixers and chemicals. All her possessions fit within her vehicle, with room to spare. She tossed on the front seat a leather bag of essential oils, balsam and frankincense and a sweet orange pillar candle she had purchased in Egypt. She felt the wind rise and the oppressive humidity seize her.

A few hundred miles away, Hanna prepared to unleash utter devastation on the East Coast. Sophie did not plan to witness it and did not know if she would even return to Watson. The same restlessness she had felt in Boston a few years ago now troubled her. The same wind tore at her soul.

She remembered how fall had ignited the trees in her neighborhood. Winter was near but not yet invasive. Respite was in the air before the familiar bone-chilling Boston winters. She had embraced the future with joy, expecting a spring engagement, a September wedding, and a house with a little studio for her paintings. Her fiancé was kind, funny and devoted. Armed with a new degree in environmental law, he was on the side of the angels in an age of genetically modified organisms. She had fallen madly in love with him since first meeting him in college. He was the only serious boyfriend she had ever known. She looked to him as the standard for any relationships. They had even discussed starting a family. It was a safe path that would let her explore life in comfort and ease.

Despite the planets aligning and the stars forecasting a great union, she felt unauthentic. Restless thoughts pecked at her peace of mind with greater speed and accuracy, eroding her confidence. She wanted to live on her own terms, stand alone with her art, and immerse herself in her painting.

Over the course of a year, the well-tended garden of her mind had grown full of weeds. Voices were stirring her in a new direction, on a path far more uncertain and rocky. She sensed that her life's journey was about to begin.

Her mother often referenced *La Tramontane* when she spoke of change. A violent and dry wind, precursor of intense blue skies and bright suns; it seasonally ravaged the land with fierce forest fires. Her mother grew up on a farm in the south of France where farmers feared and respected that wind. Sophie sat on her bed knowing that the Tramontane had arrived in Boston, full of power and wrath.

She remembered sitting in the kitchen of her parents' home, staring at an inlaid box of fragrant cedar wood. The familiar box contained four years of hope, photos, dreams and dried corsages. A life of ease waited within the cedar box. Outside laid self-discovery, transformative regrets, rejuvenating pain and freedom.

She spent three days agonizing and explaining her choice to her fiancé and her parents. She was preparing for a future now as frightening as it was exhilarating. Her college friends, out of envy or honesty, stimulated her need for artistic freedom. They cheered her on, complimenting her newfound strength. They toasted her release from the mundane.

Her family did not. They placed greater importance on the nurturing of relationships. They feared the unintended consequences of tossing and discarding love and joy. Her parents coaxed, philosophized, implored and pleaded for time to let outside influences subside.

They fought her choice, knowing that life was cruel, harsh and punitive. Sophie's decision was inexorable and absolute. Nothing could change her mind from her appointed path. She gave them three days to come to terms with her decision.

Her mother, father and her fiancé, those who loved her most in the world, had become a useless trio. They felt unwanted, recyclables at the curb, waiting for pick-up day. Rejection is never palatable. It is violent and insidious and eats at the heart long after the wound has healed. Her parents realized that they could not fill the hole eating an enormous void in their daughter's heart. They felt great pain and knew no comfort, but found in the love they bore her the strength to let her go.

On the third day, Sophie left everything behind and took a plane to Jordan to visit her college roommate. She flew 14,000 kilometers, high above the Atlantic, over Iceland and Greenland, with a stop in Paris before landing in Amman. Her late arrival in Petra postponed her discovery of the site until the early morning hours. She went to bed exhausted and exhilarated.

Eager to begin her exploration, she left the hotel at the first sign of dawn. She arrived at the main gate of the ancient city to witness the burning orb of the sun gild the crest of the hills with blushes of pink, orange and purple.

"Donkey, horse or camel?" asked a boy, keen for a sale. She declined the ride but gave the young entrepreneur the price of the fare. She knew that local Bedouin families relied on the small income to eke a living in these harsh conditions. The young boy left satisfied with her generous *baksheesh*.

The sun rose in the turquoise sky, erasing shadows. Stifling heat and scouring brightness assaulted the visitors daring the trip on foot. Sophie began her pilgrimage. Donkeys and camels, often mistreated at other tourist sites, seemed to fare well in Petra. The accented voices of tour guides and the trotting of horse and buggies passed her by, echoing in the valley.

She approached several large square cut stones marking the entrance to the sacred city. The eclectic architecture of Petra was remarkable. The Obelisk Tomb, carved in a sandstone cliff, reminded her of an Indian mausoleum transported in the Arabian Desert. Petra sat at the crossroad of caravan routes from Phoenicia, Arabia and Egypt. The site was a hodgepodge of influences she recognized from other cultures.

Sophie reached the dam reconstructed by the Jordanian government to prevent brutal flash floods. The ancient structure, unable to contain centuries of raging waters, had failed and destroyed sizeable parts of Petra. Sophie remembered reading about the tragic flash flood that swept away tourists' lives in the seventies. To her right, riders dismounted horses to view the ancient ruin. Behind her, donkeys pulling carts of speechless foreigners dashed at a mad pace to the heart of the city.

Caught by a similar fever, Sophie hurried, exhilarated by her proximity to Petra. She approached the entrance to the famed water-carved canyon *Siq* with awe. Ahead, a light blue lizard sauntered along a path once lined with Roman stones. The agile little reptile led her through the fissure. It wandered along the canyon and the myriad of earth colors painting the striated walls. She followed its lead, keeping an eye on its agile steps. The blue lizard sauntered along the water channel and through the vestige of clay pipes built by master engineers. Water had been essential to the settlement of Petra. It had brought life in the desert, grown flowers and food, kept running water in homes and lush landscapes in the now parched city. Water may be gone but the beauty of the site lingered and Sophie came upon the magnificence of Petra unprepared for the shock to her senses.

The Treasury, an impressive building facing the main route into the city, humbled all those who came upon it. Sculpted in situ, gouged out of the red, pink, white and ochre sandstone, the Treasury endured. Concealed from rain and wind by the Urn Valley, it glowed with deep reddish light. Its capitals and pediments loomed over the visitors emerging out of the canyon. Its lines showed exquisite details in the play of light and shadows.

Sophie stood motionless in front of the majestic building for what seemed an eternity.

Petra was one of the most prominent World Heritage sites. The two thousand-year old Nabatean trade city was a caravan crossroad known across the ancient world.

Merchants loaded with spices and perfumes braved the desert *en route* to wealth and glory. During four centuries of Nabatean rule, the Rose City was the capital of commerce and power. It built temples and tombs before plunging in obscurity for seven centuries.

A flock of small children peddling wares and artifacts shook Sophie out of her reverie. *Commerce is back,* she thought. A herd of tourists bussed from the nearby Dead Sea resorts disgorged from the *Siq*. They approached the rose facade of the Treasury, boisterous and loud. A tall brunette wearing expensive sunglasses and wrapped in a Dior dress, stumbled on high heels. She was trying to negotiate the terrain, but eventually gave in to the comfort of a donkey cart.

Sophie looked around for guidance and observed a young Jordanian man wearing a red *keffiyeh*. A circlet of black rope anchored it to protect his face and head from sun and sand. Wrapped in his white tunic and black robe, he leaned against a wall reading a book in the shade. He stood next to a stall offering guided tours.

"*As-salam alaykum,*" Sophie said, self-conscious of her limited vocabulary and awkward stance. She was a single young female addressing a young Muslim man in the middle of the desert.

"*Walaykum as-salam,*" was the customary answer accompanied by an inquiring look. Sophie had wrapped a scarf around her flowing auburn hair in respect. Set apart from the American tourists, she read in her guide's eyes a subtle approval.

"My name is Sophie. May I hire you for a guided tour of Petra?" she asked. Her delicate features, emerald eyes and firm gaze spoke of courage. She stood alone, unaccompanied, in the middle of the desert.

"It will be my honor," answered the young man in a formal British accent. "My name is Ahmed. I have a degree in archeology from University College and will be pleased to share my knowledge of Petra with you." His book disappeared in the folds of his black outer garment and an official ID card came out, displaying his photo and a large Jordanian stamp.

He looked at her feet and remarked, "You wear sensible shoes."

In that curious moment, Sophie sensed she had completed a silent interview and was deemed worthy of Ahmed's tutelage.

"Did you know that Petra means 'stone' in Greek?" he quizzed her, pointing to the famed Treasury and signaling the tour had begun. In a theatrical performance, the sun unveiled the uppermost heights of the cliffs exposing every nooks and crannies of the most famous building in the city.

Sophie grew up entranced by the lure of Petra. The pockmarked urn carved on top of the pediments, she knew, did not contain gold but solid stone. Yet, her bookish familiarity with the site had not prepared her for the way the sun unveiled the site's secrets.

"The Treasury was a temple. The indentations you see on both sides of the facade did not hold scaffoldings,"

Ahmed said, pointing to the narrow rectangular steps carved along the side of the Treasury.

"What are they?" Sophie asked.

"They provide access," Ahmed answered. "It is an ingenious ladder allowing the workers to carve from the top down."

"It sounds counterintuitive."

"Maybe, but it was productive. The stone cuttings form a mound on which they stood and carved a lower level," explained Ahmed.

"And they cleared the debris to access more of the facade. Clever," she remarked. "They started with the urn and worked their way down the building."

"Yes. There is so much to learn!" added Ahmed, his voice heavy with longing. "Archeologists have excavated less than fifteen percent of the site."

"This place is hypnotic. It ignites the imagination," nodded Sophie.

"It is a magnificent prize," replied Ahmed, savoring the last word. "This is where I live and where I will die. *Al Insha'Allah,* God willing."

"You mentioned the market places that served more 30,000 customers," asked Sophie. She looked at the wide expanse of ruins, desert and fiery rocks. She tried to imagine a bustling city with pools, gardens, palm trees and vibrant commerce.

"Yes, much of Petra is under tons of debris and unexplored. Finding these markets will give a human face to a city known for its tombs and temples."

Ahmed found Sophie to be a breath of fresh air from the people he met at Petra. Her curiosity was infectious, her attire was modest and respectful of his culture. She did not resemble most American women who visited Petra in tight clothing. She did not impose her vision of life on his people.

They scaled a rocky slope, framed by a daunting cerulean sky. Every step Sophie took under the brazen sun exposed her soul bare. She was shedding part of her old life for the new in waves of bliss and pain.

Petra's layered rock formations inflamed her sense of color. The lack of green hues gave the architecture a surreal parched tone to the landscape. The climatic pressure had eroded the exuberance of youth and transformed it into one of the new Seven Wonders of the World.

They climbed and met the wealth of Nabatean architecture at every turn. A few rickety café stalls, popping up along the perilous route, spoke of the gutsy entrepreneurial spirit of local villagers. Sophie and Ahmed stopped at a Bedouin's tent for refreshments. A leathery old man, wrapped in a grubby white robe, his turban off kilter, greeted them, flashing a friendly toothless grin. He sat on a dusty old carpet protected from the fervid sun by a heavy red cloth flapping in the wind. He offered respite and tea to the few exhausted travelers who dared the climb. Sophie and Ahmed accepted the hot minty beverage with gratitude.

"We are approaching the top of the mountain," said Ahmed pointing to two large formations in the distance.

"What are they?"

"Obelisks," he answered. "They represent two chief Nabatean male and female deities, *Dushara* and *al-Uzza*."

"How did they lift them there?"

"They didn't. They carved the deities out of solid rock, leveling the surrounding mountaintop around them."

"How do you know so much? You know the history of each rock in Petra. More than a normal guide," she quizzed him.

"I better know this," he admitted with a friendly grin. "I work for the Ministry of Tourism and Antiquities. We manage the Petra Archaeological Park."

"You're not a guide?"

"No, you assumed it based on my clothes. But I also own business suits, you know," he laughed.

"You should have stopped me the minute I started," Sophie argued.

"And miss a day in your company? Certainly not," he replied. "I handle the long-term management of a framework for sustainable development."

"Sustainable development?" asked Sophie, catching on that peculiar expression.

"Yes. Our management practices protect the site from the pressure of tourism."

"The negative pressure of tourism, you mean?"

"Yes, a necessary evil, but we need your tourism revenue to help the surrounding villages and towns," Ahmed answered. "Bedouin families depend on tourism for their sustenance."

"So, what were you doing on a Friday morning impersonating a guide in Petra?"

"Fair enough," he agreed, revealing a playful smile. "Today is our weekend and Friday is our day of rest. It's a good time as any to shed my ministry persona and return to my roots."

"Well, I have the most qualified guide in the Middle East," she laughed. Sipping on hot tea and absorbing the view, they eventually stood up and resumed the last stretch of their journey.

They reached the High Place of Sacrifice after an arduous trek and breathed a sigh of relief. The sense of exposure was intense after the climb. The air was cooler and crisper up on the mountaintop. Sophie looked at the dramatic cliffs and realized that she was at the highest point of the site.

Sacred places, steeped deep in human experience, hold on to memories long after they turn to dust. The altar facing Sophie still held the imprint of ancient religious ceremonies and offerings.

"They smoked frankincense, held libations and performed animal sacrifices," Ahmed said, reading her mind.

"They sacrificed humans here?"

"We're not sure, but we know that they sacrificed boys and girls at a nearby site named *al-Uzza*. This place may have served as an exposure platform practiced in ancient Persia."

Sophie stood on a rock and examined her life. She had given much to the pursuit of her art and had walked away from a life of comfort and ease. It was a final step, grave and perilous.

Alone on the other side of the world, she stood by the Column of Mercy next to a young Arab wrapped in his *keffiyeh*. The pans of his robe blowing in the wind reminded Sophie of a young T.E. Shaw. She smiled and stepped into the story of her life–the quest had begun, there was no turning back.

CHAPTER 17

THE PLACE OF FILIAL PIETY

David leaned on the banister, his face illuminated by the light spilling from the house. The wellbeing of the three women and little girl sitting at Bunnie's kitchen table was his responsibility. On the eve of Hanna's arrival, the pressure mounted to evacuate them to safety.

What a change from his self-imposed exile a few years back when he had been responsible for no one. He could not recall when the weight of his solitude lifted, but it had to do with Bunnie. Her eccentricity enchanted him. Her dinners and spirited debates charmed him. He expected nothing more than friendship.

He was at ease with the young, the elderly and most pets. His little dog kept the loneliness at bay until his friendship with both women revived him. Now Marie and Isabelle had arrived into his life, bringing additional camaraderie.

He was about to cover the grill when the sight of the briquettes triggered a flow of vivid memories. He was back in South Korea, stationed at the Suwon Air Force Base, with Nari, his Filipina wife of six months.

David remembered their house with the shoes always left at the entrance. The *yeontans*, those cylinders of coal dust and glue used for cooking and heating, lit at night. Under the floor, the *ondol*, the radiant heating unit warmed the cement floor with briquettes.

He recalled comic moments of dissembling, half across the world, trying to reconcile his traditional Indiana upbringing with his past deployments. He missed the little outhouse with a pierced wooden board and the Sears Roebuck catalog hung on a rusted nail. He could still smell the beds of red hot peppers lining the roads and drying under the blazing sun. And he could never forget the grunts of his small tailed macaque purchased from a weathered street vendor.

He remembered the intelligent face of the tiny primate and the toothless grin of his handler. The wiry old man was full of greetings, bowings and catchy slogans. Money and two bananas passed hands and David took the little monkey on a leash. If his family could see him now, living the adventures they could only read in books!

His new friend sitting on his shoulder was eating fruit, making soft groans of contentment, his belly filling up with sweet mash. As he approached home, David's delight turned to dread at his wife's expected reaction. She had developed a mean temper since their marriage, often exacerbated by alcohol. Nari would balk at his impulse buy purchased for fifty dollars, excessive in peso or won.

The macaque jumped off his shoulders and climbed in a tree. A dozen children helped find his pet, to no avail. They threw stones to dislodge the monkey, but threat and bribery could not move him from his perch. The little con artist had relieved him of his responsibility and most likely returned to his master.

David had been unprepared for the pull Asia exerted on him. The anonymity he had experienced while growing up in Indiana evaporated in the Orient. He was a United States of America pilot with the might of a super power behind him. He fell in love with the Philippines at first sight, a fact that infuriated his wife. She praised American culture above all. She had even decided to westernize her face. Against his wishes, she chipped away at her racial heritage with eyelid surgery.

"Don't do this," David urged. The procedure, a surgeon told him, would cut a fold into the eyelids to create a double fold to widen the eyes.

"I love you as you are, because of who you are," he pleaded. "You are lovely. You don't need surgery."

"If I get this done, I will look better," Nari answered as if speaking to a slow child. Her quest for westernized looks was a national obsession in parts of Asia. She saw it as an investment in her future.

"An American face gives you a good job, great prospects, the right husband. Everyone knows that," she snapped.

"But you have an American husband who loves you. You are making a negative statement on your race and on your roots. You are sending a message that, unless you look Caucasian, you cannot be pretty. Please don't do this!" he begged.

David knew that he had lost the battle before the argument even began. He caught himself begging quite a lot anymore. It never helped and she did what she wanted. Her late nights drinking with male "relatives," her spending, her obsession with American pop culture pushed him away. He was losing the war.

Nari contacted the clinic, scheduled the surgery when he was off base, and paid for the procedure with his savings. David came back to a bandaged wife he did not recognize. The swelling soon receded and her face returned to its lovely and delicate shape. Her eyes looked bigger and her confidence had grown. He hated to concede it, and would never tell her; but she looked better with westernized eyes. Maybe she was right. He fell disgusted with himself for sharing her narrow vision.

Nari spent her evenings with her friends and David often took long walks alone in the city. He longed to connect with people but realized what made him unique also isolated him. He was a commodity for his wife and for those who stereotyped him as a wealthy American.

He remembered one night when the magic of the place ignited a longing that lingered with him for years. Strolling past a fragrant wood shop, he stopped and admired the furniture. An old wood carver, wearing dusty shorts and a sleeveless shirt, greeted him in with a bow and a smile. A puff of wood dust and shavings followed his every step. On the sidewalk, near the door, two young apprentices carved elaborate flowers in a single stroke. A boy with a bandana wrapped around his mouth and nose stood in the back of the shop sanding pieces of wood. They bowed in a friendly and respectful way that restored David's spirits.

He was always smiling, bowing and returning greetings. The respect shown to elders connected with his own sensibility and clashed with his wife's lack of respect for her older parents. She loved American pop culture, fast food, fast cars and the worship of youth. They were on two separate trajectories before they even left the Philippines. He loved the traditional culture of Asia; she yearned for the disposable, the flashy and the inauthentic. Six months into his marriage, David saw the fabric of their union fraying fast.

Leaving the wood carver shop, he came upon a performance on a side street that captivated him. A single vocalist, accompanied by a barrel drum, performed a traditional Korean pansori folktale. The Song of Shimchong read the pamphlet.

David later learned that the epic tale was one of five remaining pansori performed works of twelve songs. It was the story of servitude, faith and sacrifice. Shimchong was the only daughter of a blind peasant. They lived in poverty and Shimchong ventured out daily to beg for meager scraps of food to support them. She sold herself as a sacrifice for three hundred bushels of rice and was thrown off a high cliff into the sea. The powerful Jade King saved her and she woke up inside a lotus leaf. The two married and Shimchong reunited with her father who had regained his sight.

David fell in love with the Song of Shimchong when first hearing it. He later studied pansori songs but was never as engrossed as during the first raw performance. The artist's use of a fan and handkerchief helped him understand the progressions of each scene. The sounds, metered gestures and measured pace of a deploying fan enthralled him.

David walked home, his soul satiated with mysterious ages-old tales. He was eager to share his experience with his wife but the sight that greeted him was too incongruous for words. Nari, wearing leg warmers and a tight neon exercise outfit, was in the last stretch of an aerobics routine. Her off-pitch tone and grating singing accompanied Olivia Newton-John's song *Physical.* She was breathing hard and sweating profusely. David looked at his wife, turned around, went to bed and fell asleep to the sound of her inebriated lyrics.

He woke up three days later in an army base's hospital in Seoul.

"Your neighbors found you in time," the American nurse reassured him. David glanced behind her looking for Nari.

"She is back with her family," answered the doctor standing next to his bed. "There is no prevailing symptom for CO intoxication. Complaints vary even among patients exposed in the same incident. We released your wife within twelve hours. You've been here for three days."

David did not comprehend what the man in white was telling him. He knew that he was not home, and that his wife was missing. He heard the word coma but could not relate it to his present condition. Was he sleeping and traveling in a landscape of his own imagination?

"The heating units they use here are deadly," the doctor added. "They have to retire these things soon or we'll never see the end of these cases. You had a crack in your cement floor than allowed the gas to escape. You're lucky to have survived it."

David took several days to come to terms with his predicament. He waited for his wife's visits but she only came to take him back home. During his stay in the hospital, staff had done much to increase his anxiety. He needed Nari to reassure him and dispel the fears invading his mind. No standard method existed to define the severity of his exposure. He understood that the most common site of injury was the nervous system.

The doctor spoke of neurological changes. The list spelled a death sentence. Familiar conditions stuck in his mind: dementia, coma, psychosis, amnesia, and Parkinson. He had emerged from his coma, but what was next? What side effects were waiting for him? Shadows loomed large and threatening in his hospital room.

"The worst of it is the lack of balance," he called his parents who were alarmed and ready to fly and see him. "They evacuated me to Seoul where I woke up. I remember nothing else."

He left out the unsavory parts, such as his inability to control his bowels for the first few days. He hid his wife's absence and downplayed his injury. He was near the end of his tour in Asia and his wife wanted to live in America, where the opportunities, she said, were many. He wanted to stay, but military orders called them back home to Nari's undiluted joy. They were back in Indiana within a month.

David remembered the long months of physical therapy he endured following his discharge. A pinched nerve caused by inattentive nurses overseas left him paralyzed in two of his fingers. He could not sense the cold or heat. Back home, he used to press his fingers against freezing surfaces to test his reaction. He even turned the electrical dial up to the highest setting to feel something. Nothing worked and depression caught him by the throat, chocking him.

"This exercise will help strengthen your hand and fingers," his physical therapist said. "Begin by holding your hand with your palm up and your fingers relaxed. Touch your thumb to the tip of your index finger. Squeeze your thumb and finger together as hard as you can and hold this position for a few seconds. Continue this exercise using each finger in succession. Repeat three times, touching each finger to your thumb."

The nurse was speaking in tongues and David was not listening. He was despondent, suffering from an ailment no physical therapy could cure. Heartbroken for his life overseas, he could not transition back to his life in Indiana. His departure from Asia had triggered a wave of depression that threatened to engulf him. Oblivious to his distress, his wife had connected with a group of expats and spent her time with them drinking in bars. He lived a lonesome life he did not embrace and could not stand.

Physical therapy did not restore life in his two fingers. Instead, he turned to his piano and his love of playing to restore his digits. He began to play for hours at a stretch. He played classical music–Beethoven, Mozart and Debussy–to help him regain feeling in his fingers. Over several months, David learned to play with three fingers, playing often and for long periods. He visualized his fingers dancing along the keys and imagined the blood surging through his numb digits.

Alone at home, as he was on most nights, he willed his hand to be whole again and his fears to be gone. Patience paid off and feeling returned to both fingers after months of practice. As life would have it, having gained the ability to play with three fingers, David had now to learn to play with five fingers again.

His military career ended, his life in shamble, he finally looked at his wife with open eyes. The green-card sham of his marriage was ending and the spell he had lived under for years was lifting. The instant attraction he had felt for her had dissolved into contempt. He was at a crossroad and accepted a work transfer to the Carolinas to regain his sense of worth. He gave Nari one more chance to come with him and save their marriage. She remained affable and heard his proposal. "Let's go to bed and celebrate," she said, using her favorite tactic. They fell asleep without a firm commitment, but David was optimistic. The tide was finally turning.

He came back from work the next day to a deserted home. Dirty boots had trampled the snow in front of the house and a vehicle had run over his mailbox. He opened the unlocked door and stood in the hallway facing devastation. The garish furniture Nari had purchased was gone. Missing appliances, including his oven, left large gaping spaces on the kitchen walls. He exhaled and set his groceries bags on the tiled floor, shell-shocked.

His computer and stereo system were gone. She had left behind the carved furniture he had bought in the Philippines, the carved eagle and the two large shellacked turtles he bought in Korea. David walked through his home, dazed by the scope of the theft, refusing to notice the largest missing object. His music books lay trampled on the floor, pages tattered, covers torn, marred by muddy boots. His grand piano was gone.

A murderous rage seized him. Nari did not enjoy his playing and always made him stop when she was in the house. She had no interest in pianos but she knew their value. She knew the place it held in her husband's heart. David picked up his car keys, his heart bursting with hate, when he realized that he had no place to go. She never shared her contacts with him, certainly not her whereabouts.

CHAPTER 18
PURPLE LILY PADS

They woke up at dawn, their stomachs in knots, thinking of the approaching storm. Bunnie had invited her friends to stay over one more night. David who had packed and secured his house inland stayed and gave a hand. Marie was ready to evacuate and helped secure Lily Lane.

Sophie felt the oppressive nature of the storm affect everyone's mood and sprang into action. She learned from Bunnie that there was little that a whisk and a bowl of multicolored eggs could not fix. She grabbed leftovers in the pantry, fresh vegetables from the garden, and whipped a colorful frittata. She called her friends to the table where they could review their evacuation plans over breakfast.

Dawn ignited the Intracoastal Waterway in a breathtaking palette of pink, blue and purple. Isabelle was sitting in the bay window with Dood who had adopted the role of pillow. She applied large dabs of paint to one of Sophie's canvases. In the midst of the move and the frantic news coverage, the little girl remained calm and playful.

"She's gained so much courage and resilience," Marie told Bunnie. "I have tried to shield her from everything since her father passed away, and we have both grown timid and weary. Here we are, in the midst of hurricane, a treasure hunt, felonies and she takes it all in strides."

They had all wondered about Isabelle's dad but had not asked. Mother and daughter never spoke of him. They had imagined a painful divorce but certainly not death.

"What a tragedy. I am so sorry for your loss," Bunnie whispered, reaching out and holding her hand. "She is a strong young lady. She has her mother's strength."

Marie felt undeserving of such praise. She knew the choices she had made to survive and they were not heroic. Her new friends gave her a mantle of fortitude she did not deserve. To share her secret could rip out a part of her she needed to face the daily chore of living. Widows often wore their status with singular poise, a badge of pain and courage. Hers was a badge of shame she kept alive to justify her existence in this world. She carried the mark like an anchor in the bay of her memories. Not too close, but never too far.

Marie closed her eyes at the memory and Bunnie's home disappeared. The crisp air of a splendid northern fall replaced the humidity of the Carolina weather. The summer was ending in Pennsylvania. Summer tourists were returning to their homes in New Jersey, New York or Connecticut.

The cottage on Lake Wallenpaupack had been in her family for generations. Her great-grandfather Maurice built it in the late twenties. The vacation home was large enough to house a party of ten in comfort. Her siblings also vacationed there, taking turns during the summer. Her sister Carole always vacationed there in June and her brother Philippe liked July. Marie favored August and early September.

The man-made fresh water lake was one of the largest in the state. It boasted fifty-two miles of shoreline, most of which she had explored in her youth. It was now her daughter's turn to build summer memories. She yearned for her to enjoy a beloved family tradition that anchored each generation to the land.

Marie believed in the value of unscheduled free play for children. Isabelle had rolled in puddles of mud from a young age. She was a fearless tomboy, adored by her father and encouraged by her mother. Twigs provided an opportunity to learn mathematics. Ferns and moss taught her botany, and white-tailed deer illustrated biology. By the age of three, the intrepid girl could name an impressive list of plants and trees. There was not a lesson that nature could not teach her, her husband always said, and his daughter was an apt pupil.

Marie found in her connection to the cottage a lifeline to ward off the frenzied pace of city life. Wallenpaupack was her tie to sanity. The race to success came at a price she was not willing to pay. She yearned for the sounds of the forest in the early morning hours; the ominous noises the frozen lake made in the depth of the winter; the majestic flight of the red-tailed hawk. Her heart called this place home.

Her husband Mark had wrapped up his fifth documentary, featuring Pennsylvania coal barons of the Gilded Age. He spent the summer mimicking Twain's drawl. "What is the chief end of man? To get rich. In what way, Marie? –dishonestly if we can, dearie; honestly if we must."

His appetite for life continued to delight her and his sharp mind never ceased to impress her. The Coal Barons film had upset predictions that year for the Academy Awards for Documentary Feature. Mark had won several awards before but this was his first time in the big league. They were coming home to a fall lineup of lectures speaking engagements and interviews.

"To hell with the pleasure of being a nominee," he often said. "What a bunch of malarkey. I want to win!"

Marie's latest book on High Renaissance Italy was making the academia rounds. It had secured the renewal of her tenure at the exclusive Girls' Kensington Hall in Manhattan.

Marie enjoyed the ease of her life. She had never endured hardship, toxic relationships or vicious bosses. Her home and work brought her joy and stimulated her. She married her college sweetheart, secured a great job after graduation, and welcomed Isabelle with passion. She knew that most people paid harsher dues and faced greater odds than she ever did. She remained unblemished and untested, living in gratitude and abundance.

They drove to the lake each summer, eager to enjoy nature and reconnect with each other. Her family cottage was perched on a hill overlooking the dark waters. Nearby, a brook the Lenape Indians called "the stream of swift and slow water" fed into the lake. Swift was her life in the city and slow was the pace in the country. *Summer homes have a way of inspiring dreams and restoring the balance in the universe,* she thought.

Lake Wallenpaupack was still a destination for travelers reliving their childhood vacations. They flocked to the Poconos, undaunted by the crumbling infrastructure and the aged accommodations. Vacationing there was returning to the fashion faux pas of the eighties. It was going back to avocado appliances and dusty rose commodes. It was relishing the past in a future careening towards the disposable.

Her family cottage wore its musty mantle like a badge of honor. Marie loved the old wood panels of the living room. The entryway, littered with fishing poles, wicker baskets, and nets, awaited anglers. Old black and white photographs lined the walls. Her father, her uncles and her grandfather smiled and displayed their catch. She could identify largemouth, rock bass, muskellunge, northern pike, pickerel, rainbow trout, catfish and yellow perch.

Layers of scents, sounds and tastes wove an organic cloak of memories. They linked her to her childhood and to the children before her. In the cottage, she escaped her busy schedule and focused on her family.

She looked at Mark with a renewed sense of place. He was her anchor, her constant, her lover and the father of her bright girl. The evening before their return to the city, Mark had called them out for a ride in the canoes. She still remembered that call and his voice so full of life and energy. She secured a life jacket on her squirmy daughter and settled her into Mark's canoe. He took the lead, paddling at a leisure pace. Their laughs and animated conversation bounced across the water.

Marie saw her husband and daughter gain speed, gliding towards Isabelle's favorite spot. She heard her child squeal when she realized where they were going. They reached a meadow of lily pads amidst a dark and ominous lake. Mark always took that corridor for his daughter. She loved to see the flowers part in front of her as in fairy-tales. She looked at her dad with sparkles in her eyes: the hero of her own journey to mysterious places.

"Look!" she pointed out to the secret path. "Magic!"

He paddled through the watery meadow slicing a narrow passageway that she tried to follow. Afternoon clouds turned a threatening grey. The breeze increased and the lily pads bobbed up and down on the waves. They formed a large swell hiding a wrathful lake.

Before she could alert her husband, an object bumped the right side of his canoe. Startled, she saw Mark jostle back and forth and heard Isabelle cry out in fear. Something was wrong. Marie paddled frantically through a dense mix of lily pads, stems and floating debris.

She saw Mark's craft overturn and her daughter disappear in the lake. She looked at the dark waters in shock, unable to breathe. A second later, Isabelle bobbed back up supported by her life jacket. She was thrashing in the water, entangled in large underwater stems. Massive lily leaves covered her child's face, obscuring her vision, triggering a wave of panic. Her child tried to wipe the frigid wet pads away with frantic grabs. Her screams grew louder.

Mark trashed in the water unable to stay afloat without his life jacket. Marie could not understand what was happening to him. They traveled this narrow finger of the lake often. It was an easy outing and Mark was an outstanding swimmer.

"Wait, sweetheart," Marie called out, her voice snapping. "Mommy's here. Just grab my hand. Now, love!"

At the sound of her mother's voice, Isabelle stopped screaming and stared in her direction. Marie reached out to her child and lifted her, one-armed, into the canoe. She squeezed her little girl, removing the crushed blossoms and pads from her face. Tearing off her shoes and parka, she scanned the surface of the lake.

"Listen, sweetheart. Mommy's got to get daddy, so please hold on to that paddle and don't move. Mommy will be right back! Look at me baby. Look at me." Marie stared at her child, wishing to imprint on her the courage that was deserting her.

Marie jumped into a miasma of stems. The lake was full of rubbish and crushed blooms in various stages of decay. Living, moving things brushed against her thighs and a mouthful of bile chocked her. She looked around to where the last water thrashing occurred, searching for Mark.

Adrenaline surging through her body, Marie took a large breath and dove underneath the murky surface of the lake. She opened her eyes to muddy waters. The purple tint of the underside of the lily pads floating above her blocked the light. Visibility was nonexistent and she could not find Mark. She went back up for air, praying that her daughter was still in the canoe.

She looked up at her little child, sitting straight in the canoe and floating away. *I am coming back, love.*

She stared at the overturned craft and knew despair. She took a deep breath and dove under, terrorized by the water drowning her husband. Marie could not locate him and time was running out. The lake cast a veil of shadows and deceit.

She was about to swim up when something grabbed her. She found him!

Marie seized her husband's arm and tried to pull him towards the canoe. He had been underwater for too long. He could not survive much longer and was too heavy to drag toward the surface. Her husband was a strong man, five inches taller than her, fit and toned. His body was in the throes of agonizing pain, his lungs filling with water. He grasped at life with the strength of several men.

Mark dug his nails into Marie's side, pulling her to him–out of reach of air and hope. He grabbed her shoulders and with each tug reached for his salvation. Disoriented, struggling to survive, Mark held on to his wife in a deadly embrace.

Marie fought to regain control of her breathing and quiet the panic strangling her. She resisted the urge to open her mouth and inhale the fetid water from the lake.

Her husband's hold on her grew desperate. His will to live was instinctive and overriding.

Mark was taking her in deeper with each grab. She was running out of time. Her lungs burning, she thought of her frightened daughter waiting in the canoe in mute despair. Isabelle could not become an orphan twice in the same day. Yet, Marie knew that one more underwater struggle would kill her. She had reached the point of no return, the moment that would define her forever.

Marie grabbed her husband's right hand and bit hard into the flesh, into the bone. Mark was killing her. She sunk her teeth into his arm with renewed fury and sensed him release his hold. A sudden flash of pain coursed through his body. Blood colored the water. He let go of life staring at purple lily pads.

CHAPTER 19
THE URGENCY OF NOW

Bunnie stepped onto the front porch to get a breath of fresh air. An oppressive doom weighed upon the city and the morning news did nothing to calm her fears. They had watched Hanna unfurl her plague on the Caribbean Islands. The storm had gouged a path of destruction through the old streets of Puerto Rico. Water poured inside homes sweeping away furniture, wrecking decades of family history.

Personal uploads of the devastation created a glut of information on the internet. Home videos saturated the media and made the disaster all too real, the fear palpable. Uprooted trees, boats piled up on top of each other and overturned cars created a theater of the absurd. Desolation struck everywhere, hit everyone. The storm had moved past the islands and barreled up to the Carolinas, to her home. Bunnie stepped outside to escape the barrage of images assaulting her.

She braced herself for the complete destruction expected to follow a Cat 5. Shaking her head in disbelief, she cursed the incredible poor luck that would have her pick up the pieces at her age. She had not paid her property insurance premiums since the wind and hail reclassification. Her proximity to the Intracoastal Waterway had quadrupled her payments. Life was a financial burden she could scarce afford on a good day, let alone on a cataclysmic one.

She looked at her fowl clucking in the backyard. Her goat Rosalie kept bleating in her pen and her cats only appeared now at feeding time. She was leaving her pets behind and felt guilt constrict her heart. They were on their own; their pens open for a quick escape. Chicken hawks would soon be the least of their problems.

Sophie had packed her friend's memorabilia, china, linens and silverware in waterproofed tubs upstairs. She had scanned her photographs and important papers on a small external drive. David and Marie had moved most of her family antiques to the second floor. The few pieces of jewelry she had not sold to pay bills were in her purse. They had camped at her home for the past two days getting everything ready for the great exodus. David had commandeered most of the sand bags at distribution points across town and built an impressive moat around the house. Marie and Sophie carried water and supplies to the second floor, filling the bathtubs with water.

Bunnie walked to her garden for a final harvest of peas, tomatoes, green beans and peppers. She picked up her garden's bounty in a defiant gesture. She felt an acute sense of loss. Nothing was forever, she knew, but to lose her house and livelihood now was more than she could bear. A lifetime spent caring for her home, her land and her pets, a lifestyle gone. She walked the grounds once more. Each object spoke to her; her long abandoned crab traps, her fishing poles and her garden tools. She found a knife at the bottom of a metal bucket, rusted, its blade dulled. She picked it up and placed it in her jacket pocket, feeling the warmth of the yellowed ivory handle conjure up memories.

The tool transported Bunnie to the edge of a familiar causeway. A wooden path meandered through the marsh leading to an island and a black and white lighthouse she had loved as a child. She often went there crabbing with her father and her brothers, trying to keep up with their long strides. Her father's voice always rang full of joy and life.

"Come Bunnie, let's bring home a treat to Mother," she heard him say. "You know how she loves her blue claws!" She learned crabbing when very young and still remembered her father's lessons. By the age of eight, she could fill a bushel of claws faster than her siblings could.

Bunnie was respectful of her surroundings and always released female crabs carrying egg sacs. She was a quick study and knew better than to eat a dead crab, as her brother had tried one summer. Her father had warned them against these animals' ability to release poison when dying. It rendered their flesh inedible. Bunnie was full of survivalist knowledge.

She remembered fishing on the rickety bridge before it collapsed into the marsh. Back then, tramways brought city folks to the ocean for the summer. The rite of passage long gone, a trail of oyster-encrusted pilings was all that remained of the structure. Locals did not go the beach when seasonal herds of tourists flocked to the sand dunes. Instead, they looked to the ocean as another convenient way to eke out a living from their surroundings. They went seining, fishing or clamming and harvested oysters, in the fall and winter, to sustain their families.

Nature was not a passive pursuit but a life lesson she was eager to learn. The only Dupree girl, she had over the years gained profitable skills by paying attention. She had a knack for finding the best spots in the brackish waters of tidal pools and marshes. She enjoyed teasing the shy crustaceans out of their hiding places.

Bunnie had loved to show off, as children are likely to do under their parents' watchful eyes. She had long learned the basics of crabbing and remembered her father's advice.

"No open-toe shoes," he always said. "Spot a blue crab and place your foot on it to keep it from moving."

Grabbing the flipper with one hand, he always urged her to go on. "Lift your foot and raise the crab up in the air. Never let them get a hold of you and always remember to refresh your bait during the day."

Her father kept a cooler of chicken necks for that purpose. Bunnie admired the reclusive crabs, fast on their claws. She kept her crabbing skills sharpened through her teenage years and into her married life. She used to delight her husband with her dances, always ending with a distressed blue crab in her right hand, brandishing it with gusto.

She came to marriage later than her girlfriends, who married early and were bouncing babies on their knees by the time Bunnie entered her late twenties. Her choice of husband had surprised many, but had made perfect sense for her. A literature professor teaching at the nearby college, Henry was six years her senior. Reserved and educated, from *off*, he had a sense of humor that seduced her. He was unlike the suitors who pranced in their best Sunday seersucker suits looking for attention. He was subdued, introspective, liberal, political and smart.

In her youth, Bunnie had been a stunning debutante, by northern or by southern standards alike. Ringlets of auburn hair framed her green eyes, her flawless complexion and perfect oval face. She conformed to what her social cast expected from her. She was demure, polished, conservative and aware of her standing in the community. Suitors tripped over each other to woo her. Every fall, boys lined up the county fairgrounds for a chance to take her on a ride up the ferry wheel, buy her cotton candy or win her a stuffed animal. Aloof, the belle had only eyes for her handsome plantation boy.

Sherwood Beaumont had been a contender far longer than most. His golden looks, strapping shoulders and towering height set him apart from other men. His blue eyes could melt her heart faster than a hot knife through butter, leading to many passionate kissing sessions.

He lived on a historic cotton plantation his ancestors had founded generations ago. Over the years, his family placed in conservancy over one thousand acres. Nearly one hundred acres remained for their commercial ventures. They grew pecans, peaches, blueberries and strawberries. A rarity in the South, Beaumont Plantation still farmed the land as it had done in antebellum times. They no longer cultivated rice and harvested cotton. Instead, they grew heirloom tomatoes and organic products they sold to foodies and trendy restaurants. Walking through the plantation during reenactments or taking a hayride through the property brought you back in time.

Sherwood often said that the grounds escaped torching because they were isolated from other domains. The northern forces could not find it.

"We owe our survival to their stupidity," he often said, unwilling or unable to accept that the Unpleasantness was over.

Beaumont Plantation sat on a prehistoric dune, thirty-two feet above sea level. Listed on the National Register of Historic Places, it witnessed development creep closer every year. The estate was no longer a confederate secret but a well-known tourist destination. It hosted several seasonal events, including a dazzling Christmas Special. It was on such magical winter night that Sherwood knelt on one knee and proposed marriage to his southern beauty.

Perched on a branch of the property's oldest live oak, Bunnie listened to her boyfriend's proposal with a deep sense of foreboding. Sherwood laid his name, his house, his love and his lineage at her feet in a well-rehearsed declaration. In a strange out-of-body experience, Bunnie heard the implied words woven within the transaction. To marry him, she had to set aside her ambitions, bend to her new social cast, and subdue her own independence. She was to boost her husband's ego and gave birth to babies to fortify the Beaumont line. These expectations did not surprise her as much as the rift that had grown between them.

Bunnie knew what to expect in her milieu. She considered the offer a step up from her family lineage of grocers and pharmacists. Sherwood was a bachelor most local women would love to catch. Looks and pedigree aside, Bunnie paused and recalled the overt racism that tainted everything that Sherwood did or said. When ensconced among members of his caste, he always reverted to being a plantation owner. He had injected his belief in the superiority of his race as long as she had known him– and that was their entire lives. Sherwood lived in a two-dimensional world where racism simmered and kept the status quo alive.

She fast-forwarded her life and realized that to marry Sherwood was to adopt his beliefs and pass them on to her children. The tainted legacy she would bequeath to her offspring was a deal breaker. Bunnie stared at Sherwood with a look of detachment akin to regret and stepped off the majestic oak tree, muttering words of apology. She declined his offer and left him standing in the formal garden of his prejudice.

Bunnie's world was changing and she was evolving with it. Television and the radio mounted daily assaults on her sedate life. Four black students from the North Carolina Agricultural and Technical College had begun a sit-in at a segregated Woolworth's lunch counter. The blatant injustice inflamed her rebellious spirit. Bunnie knew the South. She loved her home despite its painful and tainted history, but she could no longer wait on the sidelines to redeem it.

"They refused them service," she told her best friend Elma between classes. "But Woolworth allowed them to stay at the counter."

"The sit-ins are spreading across the South," Elma agreed.

"It is only a matter of time until they are forced to integrate public places. They can't stop this."

"You're right. A teacher told me of the S.N.C.C."

"The what?"

"The Student Nonviolent Coordinating Committee," Bunnie answered. "From Shaw University. Classes are ending this week. I know people who are taking buses to test facilities on the interstate. We call them *freedom riders.* They have a myriad of volunteers of every color. What do you say? We should go!"

Elma's original enthusiasm fizzled the moment she told her conservative parents her plan. Bunnie, who could not continue a life of unexamined beliefs, stood her ground. Despite great parental opposition, she embarked on a personal quest and rode a wave of busses during the summer of 1961. Her mother, who had made her dislike and disappointment clear, gave up trying to influence her, but did not sacrifice her safety. She made sure her daughter did not travel alone but with her school or church groups. She had not recovered from the shock of seeing her only girl refuse a Beaumont. She blamed Reverend King for her family's travails.

Over the next couple of years, Bunnie saw the world go mad. Violence and riots erupted over a black student enrolled at the University of Mississippi. Thousands of federal troops marched in the streets. Martin Luther

King was later arrested and jailed. The government unleashed fire hoses and police dogs on black protesters. Young Medgar Evers was shot to death outside his home. Four young black girls were slain in their church while attending Sunday school.

In the chaos of the early sixties, Bunnie met Henry in Washington, D.C. at a march of more than two hundred thousand attendees. Stranded on an island of concrete, isolated from her traveling companions, she panicked as waves of people pressed against her from every side. A young man she recognized from her group approached. Their eyes locked and he recognized the worry in the young woman's eyes.

"Did you get separated?" he asked. He waved his tour identification badge as if it was a law enforcement shield. "We came on the same bus and I'm lost too. I wanted to be near the podium and in the excitement I forgot our group."

Bunnie smiled acknowledging Henry's efforts to put her at ease. She had recognized him from their eight-hour trek up north. She relaxed at once in his presence. She had taken him for a student, but soon realized he was a young professor. His tweed jacket and shirt branded him as an intellectual. His friendly smile reassured her and she accepted his protection.

He stood by her at the rally, making sure she was always near him. He could smell her perfume, a mix of peony, green tea and citrus. It resembled her– floral and exotic. Henry helped her get to the top of the steps leading to the Lincoln Monument. She was supple and delicate in his strong arms. He held her tight against the human wave pressing on all sides to catch a glimpse of Martin Luther King.

She guessed the gathering was historic and the speech memorable; but it took her a while to realize that she had attended one of the most important events of the twentieth century. She had only eyes for Henry. They walked for hours throughout the capital city, transformed and lost in each other. They rode the bus back home to their respective towns and soon discovered that they could not be parted. Henry transferred to Watson that fall, and they married a few months later despite the bruised sensitivity of Bunnie's mother.

Her married life never brought the babies she and Henry wanted. Instead, the brightest mind she had ever known, the sweet, soft spoken, passionate, funny and gentle soul she had loved at first sight died of brain cancer within a few years of their marriage.

The poisonous tendrils of pain no longer invaded Bunnie's every thought. The memories of his passing and the four decades she spent alone had softened the edge of her sorrow. Her Southern spirit, resilient, graceful and indomitable had risen to the challenge.

Holding her little ivory knife, Bunnie remembered the last time they played the Fortuna game. It was a play of light and darkness, joy and grief, laughter and tears. She had been in a mad temper that day, returning home from his chemo session, exhausted and drained. To ease her mood, Henry began the lighthearted diversion they often played, but his wife would have none of it.

"Poison," she snapped at his tender words.

"Chimera," he winked.

"Baldness," she retorted.

"Funky hats," he smiled, readjusting Bunnie's hand-knitted cap on his head.

"Fear," she dreaded.

"Laughter," he replied.

"Loss," she cried.

"The Urgency of Now," he answered, taking her in his frail arms.

"Love," she rebutted.

"You," he murmured.

On the eve of Hanna's arrival, Bunnie felt the same grief strangling her. She thought of her husband and his grace in dying, his drive to insulate her from his pain and his courage. Ominous waves paralyzed her with a sense of dread. She feared she could not survive this storm, not without Henry. Her loss was as recent as the day he left her.

CHAPTER 20

THE EYE OF GOD

Gathered around the television set, Bunnie, Sophie and Marie watched the weather channel for updates on the mega storm. Hanna was on a direct course for Miami as a Category 5. Forecasters expected her to strike and lay waste to one of the country's largest metropolitan areas. She was so colossal that her cone of probability threatened the entire eastern seaboard. Bracing for the worst, the president of the United States had shortened his visit to France and was returning to Washington D.C. to oversee emergency preparations. Hanna was a monster, labeled the storm of the millennium by reporters. She was feeding off the warm waters of the Atlantic, sucking the air out of the airwaves. She had inflamed the international news media with her unquenchable gluttony.

Unperturbed, standing on the tarmac of Grantley Adams Airport, in the Barbados, Joe McGrady and Michael Reese were ready to fly in the middle of the hyper storm. Next to their towering plane, they struck the perfect pose for TV crews. The friends and colleagues enjoyed the attention. The National Oceanic and Atmospheric Administration was sending them out to collect more readings. Before embarking on their mission, they gave good press for NOAA. They had a knack for sharing complex weather phenomena with the public. They flashed easy smiles, wrapping up a routine interview with a perky journalist. The pair had given dozens of those briefings before and always provided witty sound bites to the media. They were seasoned hunters with a long line of red stickers dotting their plane, celebrating each successful hurricane mission. Together, they had clocked more than eight hundred hours of flight and flown through dozens of hurricanes. Yet, McGrady could not shake his anxiety.

"What's this pink sheet for?" asked the correspondent, pointing to Reese's clipboard.

"This is our body count contact list," answered McGrady, filling out the forms, "to notify the next of kin."

"But you must have parachutes on board," she asked, surprised.

"Where we're going, darling, a parachute won't do us any good," he said, flashing a smile.

McGrady's blue eyes and cheery disposition matched the bright Barbados sky. He was looking forward to his date with a spirited flight attendant later in the evening. Two hurricanes in one day, he smiled.

The takeoff was smooth and the mission routine, despite the accumulating cloud cover, dark and ominous. They had encountered plenty of Cat 4 storms in the Atlantic. Everyone on board was expecting good tidings. The crew was in high spirits. It was Friday and payday–a splendid combination. A few hours and they will be home. He planned to play disk Frisbee for a few hours with his golden retriever Aramis.

They encountered their first major turbulences earlier than expected on the outskirts of the storm. What had been a routine mission with a couple intense upsurges was turning into a full-blown nightmare. Hanna lashed out wind, thunder and rain at the plane with increasing fury. The light banter ceased as the crew prepared to penetrate the eyewall, the most dangerous part of the hurricane.

Black clouds, thunderstorms and outrageous gales forbade entry. The wall rattled the fuselage, weather instruments banged on shelves, and two large monitors crashed on the floor despite their padded restraints. Above, torrential rains slashed at the plane. Below, the surface of the ocean surged in anger, whipped in murderous frenzy. Lighting illuminated the cockpit and the tense faces of the pilots. The plane shivered as the pressure plummeted and crushed the fuselage. G-forces engaged in a macabre dance, vibrating in destructive sequences. Hanna, the mad cosmic conductor, lifted colossal updrafts from the sea.

None of it felt right to McGrady who reported to Grantley Adams. They had penetrated the eyewall at 1,500 feet. It was too low, he realized. He knew they could manage a Cat 4 or 5 but something unsettled him. A glance at Reese revealed his co-pilot tensing. His friend never stressed, even during their most difficult missions. He thrived on adrenaline and danger. His behavior was peculiar for a man always the most relaxed in the worst of storms. The foreign look his copilot gave him–a look of surprise and pain, sadness and prophesy–alarmed him. He sensed the danger and anguish waiting for them on the other side of the eyewall. What they met inside the eyewall left them breathless.

"We're getting through with a penetration at 1,500 feet in a Cat 5 storm," radioed McGrady, his mouth dry and his voice raspy.

"We've got 25 mph updrafts and downdrafts. Sustained winds now at 170 mph gusting to 199 mph. Pressure plummeting. Down 820 millibars," he said, grasping the enormity of their situation. They came in for a Cat 4 and instead penetrated the eyewall of a hyper Cat 5.

Since modern weather recording, only two Cat 5 hurricanes had hit the continental U.S.: the Florida Keys in 1935 and Mississippi in 1969. Over the next decades, these mega storms had framed the lives of coastal residents with painful cautionary tales. Hanna was one of those monsters, and McGrady, Reese and the crew were flying in it. An explosion shook the fuselage, followed by a second and third blast and the incredible tensing of the plane.

"We've got fire coming out of number three and four! One and two!" yelled Reese, looking in horror as the flames engulfed the plane on both sides. The Gulfstream jet kept his trajectory and speed and erupted out of the eyewall into the center of the eye in a fiery burst.

At once, thunderstorms, heavy winds and darkness lifted and blue skies illuminated the cockpit. A rink of towering dark clouds capped by foam of white clouds enveloped the plane. The eye was small, the danger gigantic and the view magnificent.

Such bliss and peace in the middle of chaos awed McGrady. He was dead, along with his childhood friend Mike and the entire crew. He had killed them on a routine mission, tempting fate. They should have penetrated the eyewall at a higher altitude. It was a stupid mistake, looking for truth in the midst of chaos. He needed strong readings to predict the exact path of the hurricane and he had sacrificed the entire crew for his quest. An indescribable sadness seized him. He ignored the sense of unfairness and rage boiling inside of him.

Seconds stretched into hours with the elasticity of fate. He grieved for his crew, for life unrealized, for his parents, and for his faithful dog waiting home, his Frisbee at his side. Joe beheld the face of God and closed his eyes as the plane exploded in a burst of fire.

Hanna was now less than a few hundred miles offshore, barreling towards the Carolina coast.

CHAPTER 21
EVACUATION

The Bunnie Evacuation Express traveled in a tight caravan formation. Sophie led the way with her new hybrid, followed by Bunnie in her Pontiac and Marie in her crossover. David was closing ranks in his red Honda.

"Why don't we pile up in my car and drive together?" Marie asked before leaving Watson.

"We need the cars to transport what we want to save," David answered, packing Bunnie's last tapestry suitcase in her trunk.

"Pack what can't be replaced; you can always buy everything else," he said. "We're going east to my cousin's cottage in the mountains. He is out of town with his family. We'll have space and be out of harm's way."

The governor had issued mandatory evacuation orders eight hours ago. They had since boarded Bunnie and Marie's homes and secured their property. The cats had disappeared the previous night and no amount of coaxing or treats bribed them back home. David had secured Rosalie in her pen with extra food and water. The fowls roamed the grounds, unable to stop their nervous clucking. Each vehicle contained five gallons of water, emergency supplies and provisions for the road. With time fleeting and their window of opportunity fast closing, they boarded their vehicles with a heavy heart, unable to articulate the dread that seized their souls.

They drove away with a last look at Bunnie's home, imprinting the image of the beloved house in their minds. Soon, they met police officers at every intersection, forcing the traffic up north. Their evacuation convoy moved unimpeded, up the highway ramp and along a steep curve. Once on the interstate, they came to an abrupt stop. A band of cars, stranded on the highway, resembled a multicolored snake sunning into the arising. They took the better part of an hour to move half a mile. State troopers blocked exit ramps and funneled the cars along the clogged artery. Once engaged on the highway, it was impossible to turn back.

Marie looked ahead for Sophie and Bunnie's cars. She glanced at David in her rearview mirror for reassurance. At least they wouldn't get separated at this pace. Isabelle rested on the back seat, headphones on, watching her favorite movie. She was holding onto to David's little dog for comfort. Marie thought it a considerate gesture on his part. Dood had a calming effect on Isabelle. The storm was overwhelming enough for adults; she could only guess the effect it had on children.

We are stuck in the greatest evacuation in our nation's history, she realized.

Marie turned on the radio and heard the shrill voices of irate drivers.

"I've been in my car for four hours and we've only traveled *three* miles," came in the voice of a caller unable to carry over the strident screams of young children. "I have an eight-month old, a two-year old and a five-year old with me in the car. My A/C stopped working two hours ago. We need help! We're dying here!"

Marie looked in the rearview mirror and felt grateful for her peaceful child and for the cool air conditioning blowing in her car. She looked at her phone and checked on David's latest texts. He'd been sending hurricane updates every other minute.

"Hanna is heading for us. Turned east," he texted.

The storm's path had veered north and was heading for their area. She was a strong Cat 4 expecting to make it to shore as a Cat 5. Marie was restless. They had been on the road for three hours and driven ten miles. They inched along past the first clusters of abandoned cars with Florida and Georgia plates. People had left their cars behind and walked on the side of the road looking for help. Radio callers were frantic. The radio host, who had been playing to the ratings, and to the growing angst of the crowd, had lost control of his audience.

"You mean to tell me that nobody's figured out how to reverse the lanes yet? This is nuts! What kinds of clowns are running this show?"

Marie saw the westbound lanes devoid of a single car and felt her heart constrict. At this speed, they would run out of gas before getting anywhere. She turned off the air conditioning to preserve her gas and rolled her windows down. The heat and humidity engulfed them in seconds, making the ride unbearable. She looked up and saw the outer bands of the storm intensify in the south. Within minutes, Hanna unleashed her wrath on the outer banks. Marie rolled up her windows to escape the downpour. Cars pulled on the side of the highway. *They are out of gas,* she thought, looking at the gauge of her half empty tank.

"And if you think of stopping nearby, forget about it," another caller shouted. "My wife's been trying to book a hotel room but they're all booked for hundreds of miles. There is no place to go!"

The calls came in to the radio station virulent and desperate. "They forced three million of us on the road without a plan. This is insane! I'd rather take my chance at my house, but we can't turn around. Instead, I'm fixin' to face Hanna in my beaten-up Datsun. Now that's a plan for you!"

The gridlock was complete, both on the road and at the few rest areas dotting the highway. Overrun by visitors, they could no longer accept patrons. Long lines of restroom users wrapped around the buildings for a chance to go. Most facilities had failed already. Callers reported seeing passengers relieve themselves in the woods and by the road.

David's texts, reassuring at first, now prompted action. "Let's go back to Franklin," he texted. All other buildings are on lock down, he pointed, but Bunnie would have access to the art building. They could anchor there.

With no progress in sight, tempers lashed out on the radio and on the road. Ahead of the group, an old pick-up truck carrying two Dobermans on its flatbed coughed twice and stopped. The drenched dogs were in full alert, sensing the change in barometric pressure and smelling danger. Marie saw two burly men emerge from the cab. They opened the smoking hood and bent over the engine to troubleshoot the problem. They yelled at each other and soon came to blows. The lanky man threw a vicious punch and sent his small partner stumbling on the pavement.

David stepped out of his car and walked over to the brawling duo. He pointed to the highway shoulder and to their truck blocking the way. David grew in stature, his body bracing for an altercation. The men stared at him and stepped back a few paces in submissive response. They went back to their truck and pushed it off onto the shoulder of the highway.

David stopped by Marie's car with the same directives he had given Bunnie and Sophie.

"We need to turn back now. If the storm comes in early, we'll be stuck in the middle of a Cat 5 with no protection. See the exit to your right? It's unmanned. Let's move while the troopers are busy. I'm going to pass you on the shoulder. Be ready to follow me immediately. Don't get stuck and do what I do. You'll follow me first, Bunnie will follow you and Sophie will close ranks."

David took the lead and drove on the emergency shoulder unimpeded by state troopers. He cast a nervous glance in the rear-view mirror, anxious about losing his friends. They all followed the plan to the letter and inched along with him off the exit ramp and to a nearby gas station. The place was boarded and deserted. Large plywood boards nailed to the windows were spray-painted with ominous warnings. "Stay Away" and the crossed-off word *Hanna* covered several windows. Fear was palpable. The cautionary words, a superstitious warning, provided a weak and desperate spell against annihilation. Marie wondered where all the people had gone. Were they boarded up inside? Had they already evacuated? Rain lashed at them from all sides, icy and fierce.

"People are switching directions and getting off the highway," David said. "Let's leave our cars here. We need to empty Marie's car of everything but food and water and drive back to the Franklin Building." He kept his voice calm, to stay his nerves and reassure Isabelle.

Marie exchanged her containers of photos and family memorabilia for three live beings in need of help. They crammed into her car and left in a torrential downpour. David, used to treacherous Indiana winters, was an experienced all-terrain driver. He took the wheels and Marie rode next to him. Isabelle and Dood were nestled between Sophie and Bunnie.

Destruction was more visible on the secondary roads. They drove blind amid chaos. The outer bands of the storm intensified, getting closer to the heart of Hanna and its fury. Around them, pine trees broke like twigs in strident blasts. David managed to avoid them, but Marie questioned their continued good luck.

In the back of the car, Bunnie sat subdued and silent, unnerving everyone. She was the matriarch-in-residence, keeper of local wisdom and safe passage. Instead of displaying her usual grit, she appeared shell-shocked. Immured in her silence, Bunnie remembered the storm of her childhood. The same electricity crackled in the air and the familiar barometric pressure plummeted. She felt the unbearable crushing of land, air and sea. She could not articulate the fear surging like a full moon tide inside her. Hanna was a threat that she could not articulate or share with her friends.

CHAPTER 22
SHELTER IN PLACE

The glass dome of the Franklin Building shone a beacon of light in the storm. Still illuminated at the late hour, it resembled a lighthouse calling in lost souls to safety. Following the sight of the art building, David avoided an impassable Fourth Street, took a turn on Fifth and was blocked on Myrtle Road. The wind and rain slammed into the car with murderous frenzy, slowing its progress.

"Charlotte Court," Sophie suggested. "Let's get to the loading docks. There are no trees there."

David took a right, inched the car in the alley, past the dumpster, and parked in front a steel door. Outside, wind gusts pounded on the metal container with the rhythm of a frenzied orchestra. Loud and menacing, the vibrations drove spikes into their brains, immobilizing them. What were they thinking? Leaving the protection of their vehicle to brave *this*?

"Let's move. We can't stay here and face the storm in the car," David urged.

Marie felt a clarity of purpose she hadn't experienced since her losing her husband. Before anyone asked her for the code, she left the shelter of her car, serene in the midst of mayhem. It had taken a hurricane to shake her inertia and the crippling fear of the past few years. Whipped by the tempest, she grabbed the hood, steeled herself against the elements and walked to the building. She reached the security padlock, punched five digits and gained entry to the loading dock. Her friends followed within seconds; David carrying Isabelle and Sophie helping Bunnie. Dood's notorious dislike for all things wet propelled her ahead of the group into the rotunda where she shook her sodden coat with abandon.

From the safety of the old building, they saw a campus ravaged by rain and wind. The two-hundred-year-old magnolia had fallen on the marble fountain and crashed the school's famed landmark. The exposed roots of the tree mimicked garish hands reaching out from the earth. Campus lights were still on, their metal poles jerking back and forth. Beams of light illuminated the darkness and unveiled the mayhem growing around them.

Guarding the entrance of the school, the grand oaks refused to budge. They had watched over the grounds for centuries and kept their protective stance. They stood by the window mesmerized by the epic dance raging between wind, water, and earth. The winds picked up in intensity lashing out from every direction. Franklin's solid walls muffled the storm but did not isolate them from nature's fury. The campus electric poles shook, blinking desperate S.O.S calls. Street lights lining Myrtle Boulevard no longer held strong and failed in a domino sequence. Following a predictable path, the lights exploded and the grid blew up and went dark one pole at a time. Soon, the school grounds disappeared from view.

"Don't stand too close," warned David, taking Marie's hand and pulling her away from the exposed bay window.

The sheer force of the explosion stunned them. The live oaks swayed, their limbs cracking to the chaotic rhythm of the storm. The building shook and the glass panes seemed to expand and contract.

Bunnie pointed to the lawn pulsating like a giant waking from hibernation. "These roots go deep and wide."

To illustrate her point, the sustained pounding of the wind and rain began dislodging the root ball. In a few hours, the hurricane had dissolved centuries of partnership between tree and nourishing earth. In a last trembling shake, the waterlogged ground gave way and released the oaks. Yanked from their deep foundations, the sentinels met a violent end and crashed onto the art building.

"Run!" David yelled, grabbing Isabelle. Marie and Sophie held on to Bunnie for dear life. They retreated to the center of Franklin as the live oaks landed on the marble columns of the portico. Aided by tempest and squalls, the battering rams pummeled the building. The structure soon collapsed, bringing the cupola crashing to the ground. Sophie glanced back and saw the pride of Watson shatter in a thousand pieces. The historic stained glass dome rained a myriad of colored shards of glass on the parquet floor. She made a mad dash for the group.

Stress lines appeared on the brick walls, triggered by the tree roots anchored deep in the earth. Within minutes, an enormous limb sliced the old receptionist's desk in half with a thunderous crash. The frightened Jack Russell yelped and jumped off Isabelle's arms seeking refuge underneath the rumble.

"Dood!" Isabelle screamed as David scooped up the child and steered everyone deeper into Franklin. "We'll find her," he murmured to the little girl. "She's hiding and we need to hide too."

"We must stay away from the windows," Bunnie advised. She was regaining her strength and fighting back the panic that had taken a hold of her in the car. "The lounge next to the print-making studio will work. We have to shelter there."

Sophie picked up the cushions from the break room. Marie carried a few bottles of juice and water still left in the refrigerator.

"We need to stay here for a few hours," Sophie agreed. "We can't go back outside. It's too dangerous."

"There is a snack machine in the hallway," Bunnie volunteered. "I have the code to it. I'll get us snacks."

"We won't have electricity for long," David said, following the matriarch. "And we can't rely on generators. I'll look for flashlights."

David went looking for more supplies and Bunnie for snacks. She had regained her fighting spirit, and wanted to contribute to the group. "I will be right around the corner," she said, flashing a reassuring smile to her friends. Sophie had seen that smile many times before and was not going to argue. Together with Marie, she settled Isabelle and kept watch until the return of her friends.

The pressure in Marie's ears kept growing. She popped a piece of chewing gum in her mouth and shared her pack with Isabelle and Sophie. They looked at their watch, counting the minutes until David and Bunnie would return.

CHAPTER 23
ATTEMPTED MURDER

Bunnie opened the vending machine and dumped the snacks and cookies in a plastic bag. She never pictured herself a looter, but extraordinary times called for uncommon measures. She was heading back to the lounge area when she noticed a beam of light filtering under the maintenance door. The sight stopped her in her tracks. She had tried to gain access to the place for days without success. And here was the proof that this room served a purpose!

She grabbed the knob expecting resistance, and finding none, opened the door a crack. Unable to resist the urge to peek, she stepped into a well-lit room appointed with janitorial equipment. In the far end, a cinder block partition obstructed her view. Careful to avoid detection, she approached the wall and peeked around the corner. A door opened into an older room lit with beams of light. A safe stood in the center of the space and a man she recognized instantly was sweeping the vault with a powerful flashlight. *I knew it!* She congratulated herself on her keen investigative mind.

Unaware of her presence, President Holzer inspected the content of the vault. Bunnie recognized the shape of paintings in protective casing lining the far wall. She doubted the objects were part of the school's inventory. A secret safe, in a secret room, at a secret hour; she'd witnessed something forbidden and dangerous. Art on school grounds belonged in the museum and not packed inside an antique safe away from prying eyes. Such covert behavior only pointed to one thing: thievery.

Forgetting the raging storm, she concentrated on an immediate peril. A single glance from President Holzer could expose her. The threat was real and grave. Bunnie faded into a corner hoping to blend into the shadows. She had to get out of this situation now. To her left, a few feet away, she detected a cast iron gate leading to a flight of descending stairs. It had to be the access to the tunnel she had been searching. It was her only means of escape.

The president disappeared into the vault giving Bunnie the opportunity to escape. She hurried to the side door and began her descent. The stairs were rusty and rickety and spoke of old age. A few dozen steps later, her feet landed on a waterlogged platform. The smell and texture of dust, rot, moss and earth enveloped her. She had to hurry and put distance between her and her boss and hope the other side of the tunnel was open.

There was still enough light coming from the upper room to guide her way, but how long could it last? She feared the beams could not reach far into the passageway. Bunnie stumbled on a piece of rock and broke her fall by grabbing on the brick wall to her right. She dropped her bags of snacks and cookies. Her breathing became labored and her heart rate elevated.

She resembled an old gator waddling through mud. Panic churned bile in her stomach. Where did she hope to go? This tunnel was the way President Holzer went by unnoticed. His knowledge of the grounds was far superior to hers. She could not outrun him. Her fears, magnified by the bizarre place and the near darkness, paralyzed her. She also noticed that the water level had risen since she entered the tunnel. What began as an ankle-deep traipsing through mud was now calf-high aerobics. Outside, the storm raged and the rain rushed in through the bricks.

Bunnie hyperventilated and cursed her stubbornness. She brought it upon herself, being an inveterate meddler and gossip. She enjoyed weaving mysteries out of shadows and spinning webs of intrigue for her books. The beams of light she counted on to guide her inside the tunnel faded in the distance. She needed to turn back and face the music. She was losing her job for this.

Her predicament was dire and her position fast degenerating. She caught the sound of a faint splash and stopped to look but only detected darkness. She labored to breathe and fight her rising panic when a searing pain engulfed her and brought her to her knees.

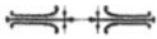

Charles glimpsed a shadow near the steel door. The mane of white hair could only belong to Dr. Wilson's sleuth extraordinaire. He took him a moment to recover from her presence near his collection. During a Cat 5 storm, no less! Would this busybody stop at nothing to spy on him? She had hindered his progress, countermanded his orders and foiled his plans. She had discovered his most secret possession. He could not let her destroy years spent caring for his art. She was insufferable and she drove him crazy.

He saw Bunnie retreat to the staircase and descend into the tunnel. *His tunnel.* He locked the door to the hallway and hatched a plan on the spot. His mind was sharp and his purpose clear. He looked around and found the object he was searching for, wrapped in black velvet. He unveiled it with care and picked up the marble hand with the same reverence he had felt when first holding it. Knowing the origin of this magnificent piece never failed to channel the legendary sculptor who had created it.

The pristine condition of his find was remarkable, unidentified and unsullied for over five hundred years. Now was the opportunity to baptize it at the altar of artistic greatness. His offering resembled the acts of plunder, mayhem, murder and coercion that often followed great art throughout history. This defining moment humbled him. No piece ever remained virgin for long; life always exacted a blood price. The secretary would pay that price. Nothing else could protect his collection.

He began the descent with trepidation. The water level had increased a good eight inches since his last trek. The flood seeped through the interstices of the motley brick wall. Flashes of light coming from the safe room bounced off his back. He did not need a flashlight. His habit of walking in darkness to avoid detection was paying off. No one had yet discovered these burrows, and he planned to take that knowledge with him to Italy. Charles was a man of many secrets: his and others'. He delighted in presenting to the world a crafted version of himself.

He heard the old secretary's belabored breaths and noted her slower pace. He was upon her and stopped to mark the moment and admire his complete lack of empathy. This insignificant pawn had dared reach his *sanctum sanctorum.* He would sacrifice her to his art. Her white hair shone for an instant, reflecting a beam of light. Fate had given its consent. He struck the back of her head with a powerful blow.

She fell facedown with muffled cry and hit the floor in a thunderous splash. It took little to end a life, he noted.

Charles wiped off the blood from the marble hand and returned it to the vault. The stubborn secretary had disturbed his plans. He had dealt with the immediate threat but her presence on campus was a mystery he needed to solve. He had planned to shelter in place at the operations center with the emergency personnel but found out he could not stay away from his art. Coming back to Franklin might not have been such a great idea, but coming back to check on his collection after the collapse of the oaks had prevented a greater disaster, the discovery of his treasures.

He now had to contend with the old secretary and the disposal of her remains. The chief had told him once that dead bodies never disappeared. Tenacious reminders of past sins, they resurfaced, creeping into the present. "It's difficult to make a body go away. They are messy, unyielding."

Charles did not relish the clean-up task and still had to solve the mystery of her presence in the building. If she was here, so might be the young grad student and Dr. Caldwell. He was sure they had noticed her absence by now. He doubted that anyone could find her, but he could not take that chance. With such pandemonium growing around them, accidental deaths were inevitable during a storm. He went looking for the rest of her friends. He planned to take her body outside during the passage of the eye, and blame her demise on the storm. Her friends would never know.

The sound of their voices alerted him to their location. He heard the anxious voice of the grad student. "Where is Bunnie? She's been out too long. The break room is not that far."

He heard the piano tuner respond. "I bet, she's testing her theory. She told us that the tunnels are part of a maze running underneath Watson."

Dr. Caldwell chimed in. "Do you think that she'd go sleuthing in the middle of a Cat 5? She looked catatonic on the ride back to the school. I did not recognize her."

The grad student agreed. "She perked up when we got to Franklin. Adversity doesn't keep Bunnie despondent for long. I bet she is trying to make good on her theory and show us off."

Charles' heart sank with each revelation, but it was Dr. Caldwell who sealed their fate. "You're right. She found the letters and connected them to Renaissance Italy and Florence. Let's send David out to look for her when he gets back with the flashlights."

Hidden in the shadows, Charles stood dumbstruck by the conversation. They knew far too much. His world was falling apart. Fear, desire, longing, wrath and panic crushed his heart.

CHAPTER 24
THE DARK PIETA

Bunnie came back to her senses, her mouth filled with muddy water and the metallic taste of blood. Waves of retching bile and blinding flashes of light nauseated her. While drifting in and out of consciousness, a thought kept intruding. She swatted it away, as she would an unwelcome insect, but it kept coming back. *Keep your head above water.* The message was insistent and pesky.

Her fingers found a small asperity in the brick wall and she turned on her side to grab it. Bunnie knew that to let go would mean her death. She was floating in a pool of mute fear when a bright light seized her soul.

She could swear she saw her mother and father pulling cotton at the dock, waving and inviting her to join in. Her brothers were coming in from the fields eager for a glass of cold sweet tea. They laughed and roughhoused with each other. The smell of pluff mud was pungent and the sound of seagulls strident and so familiar. Bunnie closed her eyes. She was ten years old again, at the lighthouse, clamming in the marsh with her grandfather. Her mother eager for the gold bullions she always brought home for dinner. Images of childhood burst in her mind with the poignancy of youth.

She recalled plucking green tomatoes from her mother's garden after the first winter nip. They sat at the kitchen table watching mother combine sugar, flour, cinnamon, salt, tomatoes and vinegar before lining the pan for her famous green tomato pie.

She blinked and found herself swaying in the old family hammock, her feet dangling off the ground. The summer breeze, her favorite book and the lingering memory of her first kiss on her lips toyed with her reality. Bunnie was settling in this comfortable state, lulled by cherished faces and places.

In the distance, buffeted in fog, her senses alerted her that none of it was real, but she could not let go. The muddy water inserted wisps of fear in her mind, scattering beloved memories. She could no longer recall the favorite sounds and smells of her childhood. She was shivering from cold.

The mustiness of the tunnel reminded her of an Italian church she visited with her students a few years back. No longer supported by papal funds, it had crumbled into darkness. Bunnie remembered her walk past the right side aisle and across the transept to the first chapel. She could hear the ceaseless chatter of the students in the front of the church and walked away from the noise, seeking solace in the ambulatory. She reached a dark alcove and used her camera to breach the curtain of darkness before her. The flash illuminated a recess from which a Madonna sprung, looking imploringly from the void. Locking eyes with the statue, Bunnie stumbled back in the aisle. The Madonna disappeared into the void, wrenching some hidden truth. That moment of brilliance was gone, the light extinguished and her hopes dashed.

The past connected with the present and she understood. The air smelled just like it did now, musty, damp, earthy and full of decay. The humidity of the tunnel and the seeping water eroding the rock brought the same sense of loss she felt in that church. She was the butt of a cosmic joke. She was drowning in muddy water, killed by a psychotic university president. *And all this over a statue.*

Bunnie knew that if she did not hold to the small ledge, she would die. She hoped for a miracle and for her friends to find her. She wanted to be the Madonna discovered in that brief flash of recognition. She felt so cold, like a statue, a lonesome marble figure forgotten and neglected. She would hold on as long as she could, hope for rescue, for a flash of brilliance that would take her out of the darkness.

Her parents' kind voices came loud and clear, welcoming her in a joyful embrace. Her beloved husband was there. She should go to them and be at peace. The pull of memories became almost too strong to resist. She was almost home!

At the edge of darkness, she saw a light probing the tunnel. She heard familiar voices call out to her. *David and Sophie!* She had to make a choice. Bunnie answered the call. Her southern spirit, so often tested and always valiant, rallied once more. She called for help.

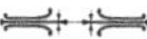

"She's been gone too long," Sophie informed David when he returned from his supply run.

"I found two flashlights and enough batteries to last us through the night. I'll go back for her now."

In light of their worries about Bunnie, David did not want to relay his growing fear for his little companion. He remembered the apocalyptic collapse of the cupola and his dog's escape through the shards of glass. He needed to believe she had survived the assault on the building. Dood had made a dash for the auditorium and survived the initial crash, he was sure of it. She was a fretful dog, terrified of loud noises and he feared for her in this pandemonium. He hoped that she would be safe, hiding somewhere; but she had not yet responded to his calls. He knew that he would risk his life for her, she meant that much to him. Dood had been with him through a decade of hardship and solitude. She slept with him on his sofa at night and she was the first and last friendly face he saw every day. She was his constant and now she was lost.

"No news about Dood?" Marie asked, sensing his distraction.

"Nothing yet. I bet she is hiding in a crawl space out of harm's way. She hates thunder and lightning."

"She may still surprise us all," Marie answered, looking over his shoulder with a wide grin. Taken aback his friend's lack of concern and jovial tone, David turned around to find out what was so funny. Stunned, he saw his little Jack Russell clear the corner.

At the far end of the hallway, racing towards her master with a purpose, Little Dood appeared. Saint or sinner, resembling the white horse of the apocalypse, she was on a mission of mercy. In a splash of daring, she came to a halt in a plucky somersault and landed at her master's feet. She was so energized that her entire body shook, lifting her above ground.

"Oh my God," David murmured sweeping the little dog in his arms and crushing her against his chest.

Dood wiggled out of the embrace and pitted herself in front of him. She barked in low tones he'd never heard before.

"She's telling us something," Isabelle said, cutting short the merrymaking and pointing to the obvious.

"Yes, look at her!" Sophie pointed to David's pants. "She is chewing at your hem. She wants us to follow her!"

Leading her friends through the dark corridor, Dood ran to the maintenance room. She stopped in front of the door and renewed her barking. David's beam of light flashing on her white fur transformed her into a bouncing halo.

"She must have found a way in," Sophie said.

"How?" asked Marie shaking the locked door.

"Not sure, but we must take the door down," David answered breaking a glass panel. He grabbed a fire extinguisher and looked at Marie. "Please go back to the lounge area with Isabelle and Dood. Sophie and I will take a look at this room."

Marie walked her little girl and Dood back to their shelter. From the relative safety of the lounge area, she heard loud bangs of metal on metal. They punctuated her thoughts and unnerved her. *Where is Bunnie?* She settled her charges on the sofa, plugged in a new movie for her daughter and nestled Dood in her arms. The battering of the door had ceased. *They've gained access!* The building became still and quiet. The sound of the freight trains was gone. She guessed the eye of the storm was passing over Watson.

In the chaos unfurling before her in a mad tango, Marie felt her strength return in waves of joy and sorrow. Watching her daughter's demeanor during this turmoil taught her resilience and hope. Life would always bring heartbreaking moments–experiences that brought people to their knees in capitulation. The strength to endure it resided in the individual's ability to forge links with others. In the eye of the storm, Marie found the peace she had searched for so long. She knew that the eyewall was but a few miles away, ready to strike again. But in the stillness of the moment, she found the courage to face devastation.

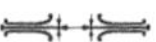

David slammed the bottom of the extinguisher on the door knob one more time. "We're getting through!" The door finally gave in and they walked into the maintenance room. David flashed the light around the space and couldn't find any clues about Bunnie.

"This is strange. It looks like a cleaning lady's closet," said David, turning to the wall and floor-to-ceiling shelves holding janitorial supplies.

"There is another door, over there," Sophie pointed to the secondary exit in the corner. She tried to open the door knob. "It's locked. If Bunnie came through, how could this door be locked on this side? She didn't have a key."

"I don't know, but I trust Dood," David answered. He inched towards the door and stepped on something crunchy and bright. Shining the light on the floor, he saw a metallic candy wrapper.

"Wasn't she looking for snacks?" asked Sophie.

"Yes, and that's her favorite candy," said David, picking up the wrapper. "Bunnie's been here. We need to take down that door."

Working in tandem, they soon got into a pounding rhythm that got the better of the second door in minutes. It fell forward with a thunderous thump. A large vault stood in the middle of the room.

"What is this? A safe?"

"Yes, and it's locked like the doors," Sophie answered, trying in the handle.

"It has to be the key to what we've been looking for. Bunnie was right!"

"And that's where she went," David agreed. His light shone towards the entrance of an old brink circular staircase.

"Let's go," Sophie urged.

"Yes, but be careful."

"Why? There is no one here."

"Who do you think locked all the doors?" David asked, beginning the trek down the rusted metal staircase.

They kept a hurried pace, treading in a foot of frigid water, careful not to slip on the brick floor. David felt something rub his leg. He bent down and retrieved floating debris, a plastic bag, potato chips and candy. He felt time slip away. His flashlight swept the walls of the tunnel and found a prostrate form.

"Bunnie!" Sophie screamed, her gaze following David's beam. He handed the light to Sophie and reached out to the frail woman, lifting her in his arms, out of the chilly water. Sophie shone the light on her dear friend. Rivulets of blood trickled down her scalp and face. She took her pulse and found a faint beat.

"Oh my God, David, she is alive! Let's take her back upstairs!" They turned back and started the trek up the tunnel and the staircase. David maintained a swift pace. Bunnie weighed next to nothing but he was careful to keep her close to his chest and avoid any bumps in the dark. The return journey took less than five minutes.

Sophie reached the lounge first and took Isabelle and Dood to the adjacent room. Marie rushed to Bunnie's prostate form. They laid her on the sofa and disinfected the wound. She had sustained a blow to the head but her cut was superficial, more spectacular than life threatening. Marie treated the scalp and bandaged Bunnie's head to stop the bleeding. They wrapped her in curtains and warmed her as best they could.

Bunnie was responsive to her name and her location, but could not recall the events of the past hour. She could not explain her presence in the tunnel or the cause of her injuries. David had shared with Marie their findings and suspicions, but he did not force the issue. They both suspected Bunnie had suffered a concussion and would need time to recover. She was warm and comfortable and they would have to ride out the rest of the storm in the lounge area. While Isabelle and Dood kept watch over their convalescent friend, David, Marie and Sophie retreated to the hallway to discuss the situation in private.

Sophie was near hysteria. "She was attacked and left to die in that tunnel!"

"Who did this?" Marie asked.

"We all know who did this," Sophie snapped. "We are well past that point."

"Sophie is right," David conceded. "But where to report an attempted murder when the police is implicated?"

CHAPTER 25
TORNADO

He shook in desperation, his fury knowing no bounds. They were at Franklin! The kid, her mom, the undergrad student and the piano tuner! Would he ever get rid of these idiots?

Charles felt utterly violated. They had spent countless hours investigating him, probing in his affairs and papers. They were nobodies and yet they had shattered decades of well-laid plans and preparations. An intense frustration coursed through him, igniting his rage. Faced with a single course of action, would he have the strength to do it? He stood petrified by the enormity of his plan and by what he could do to claim his prize. At risk was the discovery and seizure of what he held dearest in the world. What he alone had discovered and protected. His treasure required the ultimate sacrifice.

A choice he had willingly made in the tunnel with the old secretary. He had crossed a point of no return, entered unchartered territory where the dragons laid in wait.

His work was not over. His discovery would not be secure until all who knew of it were silenced. But how could he disable a grown man, two women and a child? *Divide and conquer.* The secretary's disappearance worked in his favor. Her absence was certain to trigger a search. They had to separate to look for the secretary and keep watch over the little girl. Charles had a clear choice. Only a gun could disable people fast. Hand combat was not a skill that Charles learned, he smiled. A gun was much cleaner.

His gun was in his safe on the second floor of his house. The problem lay in disposing of the bodies, but the tunnel provided the perfect hiding place until he could devise a permanent plan. The storm raging inside his mind was picking momentum. Charles heard reason, decency, and morality make a weak play for his sanity. But he was far too invested to react to mere human morals. He was beyond reason.

Outside, the storm was still battering Watson but it would stop with the passing of the eye. Expecting the tunnel to be impassable, Charles waited for the eerie calm to blanket the campus. He planned to run to his house, which was less than a block from the back entry of Franklin, and get his gun. By the time the eye of

Hanna passed above the school, he would be back to exact his revenge.

Through Franklin's battered windows, Charles glanced at his house standing tall amidst the devastation. An act of God had spared it. Trees shattered, roofs peeled off and piles of bricks littered the campus. Still, Franklin and the President's home prevailed. Hanna had not razed them.

His enemies would not experience such reprieve. Charles braced himself for the devastation he was prepared to inflict on his staff. The eye of the storm was the brief respite they would experience before their death.

The raw power of nature had fascinated him from a young age. He had always loved storms, thunder and lightning. Hurricanes were special. He remembered attending a show of photographs taken from the International Space Station. They featured the eyes of past storms. The statistics, interjected in the narrative of the show, astounded and humbled him. The total energy released by the rains and clouds of an average hurricane was immense. It equaled two hundred times the electrical generating capacity of the entire world! The winds alone could generate enough kinetic energy to power half of the planet. The majesty of such giants, the loveliness of their destructive natures stimulated him.

He recalled the amazing photographs taken by dauntless storm hunters. A picture named Sitkowski had immortalized the Stadium Effect. He remembered staring at the image depicting the inside of a well-defined eye resembling a bowl-shaped stadium. Towers of snowy clouds made up the surrounding eyewall, similar to stadium seating. The lower part, near the center of the eye, made up the playing field. In the center of the photograph, enraged waves still visible at such high altitude, thrashed the ocean floor. Reality was now imitating art. He was in the midst of a power struggle resembling the exquisite images.

The slaughter unleashed around him energized Charles. Nature mirrored the storm erupting within him. Safety resided at the heart of the eye. Strong winds converging towards the center could not reach him. As if on cue, the rain ceased, the sun shone, and the wind dissipated. Free from doubts, Charles' mind was at peace. Gravitational forces pinned him to this moment. His love and devotion for his collection demanded a reaction proportionate to the depth of his commitment. Unafraid, he opened the door and walked into the eye of the storm. He had never been on the side of the angels, nor did he want to be. He stood with the extraordinary, the brave and the undeterred.

Hurrying, yet conscious of the limbs of tree blocking his way, he walked to the back entrance of his home. On closer look, the house had not escaped unharmed. A defective hurricane shutter had let water inundate the first floor. Charles did not stop to examine the damage but ran upstairs to his private quarters.

Charles opened his TL-60 safe in a matter of seconds and reached inside for his Glock and ammunition. He enjoyed target shooting and had a pass at a local county range. His skills would serve him well tonight. His strategy was simple: distract the group and dispatch them one at a time. He planned to be gentle with the little girl. She would not witness her impending doom.

His coldness reassured him. Strength is tested in the furnace of hell, he knew. The trial was upon him. Every step he had taken throughout his life had led him to this point. He had calibrated his life to that single pursuit of the extraordinary. He had wished, believed and hoped for greatness. And greatness had been thrust upon him by one of the most famous artists in the world.

Di Lodovico Buonarroti Simoni, better known as Michelangelo, was a genius from a tender age. His relation and apprenticeship with a stone cutting family transformed his life. He was fond of saying he had suckled from his wet nurse the hammer and chisel that helped create his masterpieces. He understood statuary marble unlike any other artist. He had developed a fixation with stone and considered it the greatest medium. It far surpassed painting. An irony since his Sistine Chapel remains one of the world's greatest masterpieces.

Charles imagined Michelangelo's teen years, full angst for undisclosed yearnings, full of passion for his art. He recognized his frustration and commiserated with his vexation. To be the best of his age and view mediocrity rewarded with commissions and patronages must have been insufferable. To see others catapulted to fame for works he found substandard was infuriating. These thoughts, for a genius such as Buonarroti, must have been maddening.

He understood the artist's visceral need to sculpt his name on the Pieta when hearing it attributed to another sculptor. Charles often dreamt of living during the High Renaissance era. To come of age when art flourished like mad bougainvillea, gorged on sun in lush Florentine gardens!

He did not blame the artist for turning to forgery to increase his prospects; it had launched his Roman career. But the Sleeping Cupid was not his first forgery, as most modern art historians claimed. By the time Michelangelo sculpted it, he was an experienced forger. He had perfected the art of aging his pieces to pass them for antique works. The joke was on those he fooled. The world knew of one sculpture; Charles knew the truth. He had uncovered it and kept it hidden from prying eyes.

He heard a crash downstairs and rushed to the kitchen to see the limbs of a pine tree slam on the table. *The storm*! He had a few minutes to waste before the fury would return. His hand resting on the grip, he felt the reassuring weight of the gun in his pocket. He reached the door and saw the eye of the storm dissipate and the eyewall return with a vengeance. He only had minutes to make it back to Franklin! Charles started to sprint towards the art building with a vengeance. That's when he noticed something odd. The sun still shone on his face, but the rain had returned drenching him with sideways lashes.

He looked up and saw a dark funnel emerge from the clouds. A rotating column of air descended from the hurricane's higher elevations. He had no words to describe the merging of colors before him. Green, orange, red and yellow pulsated to a manic tempo. The air burst into primary colors. He had run out of time.

Somewhere in the back of his mind weather trivia surfaced. The little known fact that hurricanes spawn tornadoes in their wake surfaced. It evoked frightful definitions. F4 and F5 described *devastating* and *incredible* phenomena. Science qualified F6 tornados as *inconceivable.* These descriptions failed to convey the raw and numbing fear they inspired. This monster unfurling within a mega storm clashed with his sense of the rational. No other weather phenomenon matched a tornado's fury and destructive powers. He had not expected a tornado embedded in the eye. They usually developed away from the eyewall, in bands of thunderstorms and intense showers. *Not here, not now!*

Charles looked at the funnel loom above him and darted for the shelter of the Franklin Building. The colors of the sky coalesced into a black mass. The air pressure plummeted and the horns of a hundred cargo ships crushed his brain. He experienced terror and witnessed the genesis of his end.

Charles despaired for what he was leaving behind. His treasure was unprotected and his legacy shattered. The discovery of the century buried under rubble, returning to obscurity. Undiluted rage for this absurd turn of events cracked his sanity. This contrived *deus ex machina* ending was robbing him of his life's pursuit. It was unthinkable it could end now.

He looked up and shouted a primal scream of rage as the tornado lifted him in the air. He was airborne, unable to tell top from bottom, left from right. Updrafts and downdrafts embraced him, squeezing the air out of him. Debris battered him from every side. He closed his eyes to protect his sight. His hands flailing on his sides, he tried to keep his balance. A multitude of objects struck him. A serrated piece of metal drew blood. Others struck him with the blunt force of a wooden shutter. None had struck his head yet, but he feared it was a matter of seconds. He was inside a dryer full of butcher knives and nails. Tremors engulfed him. Charles felt everything but saw nothing. Taught and sensitive beyond endurance, his eardrums finally popped. His eyes crawled into the far recesses of their sockets, unable to sustain the agonizing pressure.

He suffered great loss. Not for the daughter he never knew; or the friends he never made. Not for the wealth and influence he was about to lose. He wept for his art, for his collection, for the stupid act of fate that left it unprotected. Defiant to his last breath, he let a muffled scream of hate soon erased by the sound of the apocalypse.

The scents infusing the tornado surprised him. The air smelled clean, of grass and earth, and fresh cut pine. It was as incongruous as the dented metal door that flew into his side and ripped him in half.

CHAPTER 26
UNRECOGNIZABLE

They had the gait of refugees hoisting the brutality of the world on their shoulder. Shuffling out of the Franklin Building, they were bound by adversity, both man and nature-made. Wrapped in dusty curtains they tore away from broken windows, they fought the chill of the morning dew. They began their exodus from a structure they feared had become unstable. The inside of Franklin was littered with glass, fallen ceilings and shattered walls. The edifice had survived the storm but could still collapse at any moment.

Marie and David helped Bunnie step outside. The matriarch could not stop a slight trembling of her limbs, but she insisted on walking with them to survey the aftermath of the storm. Sophie had wrapped Isabelle in a magnolia curtain and carried her. Beyond their haunted look rose strength and resilience, hope and gratitude. They held each other for comfort, seeking human warmth.

They emerged from the only pre-Civil War building left standing on campus. Large piles of red bricks spelled the demise of Watson's two oldest dormitories. The school landmarks were gone. Instead, piles of debris blocked the road and transformed the familiar into a wartime landscape.

Standing on top of the marble steps of the grand entrance, they surveyed the campus. Broken glass, shattered tree limbs and crumbling bricks slowed their exit. David and Marie kept the mood of the party light. They offered encouragement, keeping their spirits high, when an eerie sight stopped them in their tracks.

"Look mom!" Isabelle exclaimed, pointing at the street. "A washing machine!"

They turned in unison toward an old battered washing machine standing in the middle of the flooded street. A yellow placard stuck to the side urged students not to leave their laundry unattended. The sight forced them to sit down on the steps and take a pause.

"I was expecting emergency responders, but the repairman came first." David said, unable to resist the joke.

The funny remark soon swelled into a communal laugh they could not contain. In the midst of utter chaos, life surged unbidden yet so welcome.

The early morning hours turned a pink sky into a crystal blue backdrop and the sun began its ascent.

"Here and gone in less than twelve hours," Marie looked around in disbelief. "The sun is back. What an incredible tease! The sun…after this!" she said, looking at the chaos and destruction surrounding them. She sensed hysteria rise and choke her. She walked away, grateful for the old washer. It was distracting and amusing to her daughter. And that was enough to move on to the next moment, the next minute needed to compose herself.

"Years from now, the washer will be the biggest thing we remember," David predicted. "It will take on epic proportions."

"We need to figure out what to do," Marie stressed. "The water is receding but this dark syrupy muck covers the streets. I don't think we should wade through it."

"Let's wait for the rescue teams. We still have water and the snacks. We can shelter next to the downed magnolia over there. The curtains will protect us from the sun."

They ate under musty draperies while minutes turned to hours, dashing the hope that rescue was on the way.

"Listen, no sirens, nothing. No birds and insects," interrupted Sophie. "We've been here for more than an hour and my cell phone isn't getting any reception."

"Those who stayed are on their own for the first seventy-two hours, until FEMA gets here. Is that true?" Marie asked.

"Yes," Bunnie answered, exhausted her voice a whisper. "After Gabriella, we waited for help for days."

David looked around and sighed. "What is normal anymore? We need to get off campus and see if your house is still standing, Bunnie."

"We must be careful and keep an eye out for dangerous critters," Bunnie said. She was coming back to life under her makeshift tent. She appeared more alert and conscious of her surroundings. "Snakes and poisonous animals have been dislodged from their habitat and are as disoriented as we are. We need to be very careful."

"There is no *we,*" David answered turning to his friends, pleading for support. "I will get help and inspect Bunnie's house and y'all stay put."

"I'm coming with you," Sophie interjected. She left no space for discussion but they realized that traveling in group was far safer that alone. They soon came up with a strategy. Sophie and David planned to investigate and Bunnie, Marie and Isabelle were to stay on campus.

"We'll be back in an hour. The house is only four blocks away," he reassured them.

David fashioned two walking sticks out of the broken limbs from the magnolia tree. They carried water bottles, tucked their jeans into their socks and hiking boots, and headed for Lily Lane. Given the state of the campus, they didn't expect to find Bunnie's house standing. But if by a miracle it was, it contained supplies stored in the upstairs rooms they sorely needed.

Marie saw the scouting party depart, and pleaded for their safe return. She hoped for relief and prayed for the safekeeping of their houses. The things that connected her to her past, still packed in boxes, awaited her home. She froze at the thought it could be lost.

In the distance, Marie heard emergency sirens punctuate the silence. Low lying areas of town, including the trailer parks were at risk. After the last day of evacuation broadcast, she doubted that many stayed. But she never imagined she'd be stuck amid chaos with her daughter.

Marie readjusted Bunnie on the cushions they carried out of the building. Her friend had sustained a head injury, the severity of which had yet to be determined. Bunnie gazed in the distance, trying to grab a memory. She looked at the little Jack Russell who had saved her life. She still felt the rising waters of the tunnel drowning her.

"How are you doing, Bunnie?" Marie asked. "Is your headache getting better?"

"Yes, it's almost gone. I am just very tired."

Marie offered her more water and readjusted the cushion under her head. The emergency kit they found in the break room helped her clean the wound and apply first aid. The cut was in the back of her head and Marie wondered how her friend could have sustained it. She pictured Bunnie butting head first into the walls of the tunnel and suffering a blow to her forehead, not the back of her head. Yet, they found her on the ground, grabbing at a ledge to keep her head above water. The story had holes and Marie hoped her friend would recover her memory soon. She sensed something sinister lurking in Bunnie's mind.

"I am so close. I can almost remember," said Bunnie reading her mind.

"Rest, now, it will come back. It will," Marie answered, placing a wet cloth over her friend's clammy forehead.

Bunnie had been right. The tunnels existed and the strange safe they saw in the maintenance room was the clue. Her memory was the key to solving the mystery.

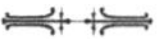

David held out his hand to Sophie and guided her around a large truck blocking the street. It laid upside down, the body mangled, the tires gone. A metal pole had pierced the gas tank, leaking a syrupy liquid into the street. A trail of gas snaked its way down the street with an oily shine. Entire rows of houses were gone, reduced to piles of rubble. Others seemed barely touched, the deeper they moved into the Old Village. They proceeded with caution, making loud noises to warn snakes and alligators of their approach. David observed two large black snakes painting delicate strokes of glistening scales across the water a few feet away. He distracted Sophie from the unsettling encounter.

David was not a man prone to fits of spirituality. His only appearances in local churches were to tune their pianos. He was always respectful of the places he visited, but he could not recall the last time he attended a service or said a prayer. But this walk among destruction and chaos unhinged him. The closer they came to the house, the more urgent his plea. He wished for Bunnie's house to be left standing. He yearned for a miracle. Approaching the last block leading to her house, David braced himself for the sight of devastation. He closed his eyes before taking another step and prayed with rabid fervor. He opened them to a gleaming house on the hill.

Sophie fell to her knees in quiet acknowledgment. Bunnie's house stood untouched among the ruble. The sight humbled her. She had until now collected experiences as the prerequisite to her maturing art. She fueled it with sensations: the loss of a relationship, the rebirth of a new acquaintance, the southern sun, the golden leaves of northern falls, the Tuscan light, or a medieval street in the city of Agen.

Bunnie was a southern legend who had provided her with a treasure trove of experiences. She had ignited life on her canvas and brought a color to her art she had not explored before. She had tucked at her heart strings–a pluck here and there to make the heart flutter, no more. Life was propelling her with great intensity towards the pyre of her art. Her experiences were vignettes, reference pieces, until now. Hanna changed it all. Bunnie made it personal and real. Running towards the house, Sophie thanked the universe for the mercy shown to a lady full of love and verve. She felt an intense gratitude fill her heart and true compassion melt her detachment. Art had become personal, bloated with pain and regrets.

"It looks untouched," David noticed. "None of the windows appear broken."

"It looks brand new," Sophie said, disbelieving her eyes.

"Yes, the hurricane peeled away the layers of paint."

"The house looks white!"

"We won't have to sand the house before we paint it," he nodded with a smile.

"The sheds are still standing," she added, surveying the property.

"If the old canoe is still in the garden shed, we can bring everyone back home in less than one hour," David pressed. He could not wait to share the good news with his friends.

The last street was blocked by a large uprooted live oak. It took David's calm and Sophie's fortitude to ignore several slithering snakes emerging from under the tree.

"We need the canoe," she hissed. She hated snakes.

"Stay close and alert. We're almost at the sandbags."

His lady friends had laughed at his doggedness when preparing for the hurricane. He had depleted two sandbag locations in the cover of darkness. His persistence had paid off and none of Bunnie's land had flooded. David walked the grounds relieved to find the house untouched.

"The house is fine. You may want to get the porch ready, while I bring them home," he suggested.

Without a moment to lose, he boarded the canoe and returned to Franklin in a fraction of the time it took them to get to the house. The sight of the canoe brought Marie and Bunnie to tears. *If the canoe is safe, may be the house is intact,* Marie thought.

David's smile and reassuring words confirmed the house had survived the hurricane. "Your house is safe Marie. The sandbags held there too."

"I need to take her back home first and I'll be back for you, Isabelle and Dood," he added. "Sophie is at the house preparing the place for Bunnie."

Marie settled her friend in the canoe and watched as David paddled back to the house. Once settled on the porch bed, with Sophie attending to her comfort, he returned for the rest of the party.

In the canoe, Marie and David paddled in silence. The sun was high in the sky, burning their exposed faces. Their last bottles of water gone, the pangs of dehydration had grown into general lightheadedness and fatigue. They kept Dood from lapping the contaminated water. They sustained hope knowing that Bunnie's clean water supplies were nearby. The canoe glided past piles of rubble and gutted homes. The destruction made no sense and jumped from one house to the next, inflicting pain or showing mercy. Marie looked at her surroundings in shock.

They approached the sandbags with care, docking in the front of the house. Marie could not believe her eyes.

"The cats, the fowls, they're all here! Incredible! They must have hidden under the house during the storm."

Dood stretched her legs on the familiar yard and Isabelle looked in awe at the water lapping at the sandbags.

"Mom! Look, we have a castle with a moat!" Marie looked at her daughter, overwhelmed by the innocence of youth, grateful for the strength that coursed through her veins, and thankful for the power of friendship.

Reunited on the porch, with Bunnie carefully attended to, they sat on rocking chairs, looking at the ocean, dazed by the impact and scope of the storm.

Birds chirping from the treetops distracted Marie. "The birds are back. I wonder what will happen now that their habitat is gone. Can they even survive a hurricane?"

"Yes, they get carried away by the storm along the coast, even inland. They are winners and losers when habitats change. Several years ago, extensive deforestation up north displaced my mom's favorite birds," Sophie looked up at the tree and pointed to the birds. "But these are not our birds. They are tropical birds."

On the highest branches of the largest live oaks, white-tailed tropicbirds screeched in agreement. Plucked out of their tropical islands by the storm, they had dispersed widely across the ocean and some had landed in Bunnie's yard. The slender white birds were still shaking off the water from their white plumage and long tail streamers. Their distinctive *keee-keee-krrrt-krrt-krrt* echoed through the neighborhood, calling out their party.

Gathered on the porch, they looked around, grasping at the miracles surrounding them: their lives, the house, the land, the history of several generations, the memories preserved and tropical birds singing in centuries-old live oaks.

CHAPTER 27

THE HOUSE ON THE HILL

They heard the sounds of rescue before witnessing the first responders turn the corner on Lily Lane. The motor of the inflatable raft hummed and stopped at intervals to let the firefighters check on the houses still standing. They called out for residents and entered the premises, sometime with axes, to search for survivors. They spray-painted a large X on the front of the house and filled each quadrant with numbers and letters.

"What's the writing for?" Marie asked, pointing to numbers and letters on the wall.

"They help identify hazards, live and dead victims, date of rescue, and who performed the rescue," David answered, facing a barrage of questioning looks from his friends.

"Five years as a volunteer in the fire service taught me a thing or two," he smiled back.

"You never cease to amaze," Bunnie said. "You were right about the sandbags."

The firefighters approached their home in disbelief, shocked to discover a homestead intact, complete with goat, guinea hens, cats and chicken and a wall of sandbags surrounding a large property. Whoever had prepared for the hurricane had done their homework. A man in his mid-thirties approached the edge of the bank and waved them in.

"Is anyone injured?" a paramedic called out.

"We are fine," answered David. "We have four adults and a child here."

"Did you stay here during the storm?" asked an incredulous firefighter.

"No, we tried to evacuate, but had to turn around after being stuck on the highway for hours. We took secondary roads back to Watson and we sheltered in place at the art building."

"You were lucky," a somber firefighter with two-day beard growth answered. "We lost hundreds on the highway. Hanna plowed right through them. They didn't stand a chance."

"Are they dead?" asked Marie.

"Yes, it was a carnage. We also lost first responders who went out during the storm despite orders when the calls came in from family and friends."

"Is your house structurally sound?" asked the leader. "It looks as if your home has been bleached white."

"You are welcome to check the buildings," David said. "We also have a friend who may have received a concussion and needs your help."

"We are paramedics," a strapping young man answered. "Take me to her."

The firefighters followed David to the front porch where Bunnie laid, attended by Marie and Sophie. Enjoying the attention of good looking firefighters in emergency gear, she offered them sweet tea and cookies from the comfort of her sofa bed. The young man smiled and retrieved a cuff from his bag and began to check her vitals.

"You have sustained a closed head injury. There is no major damage to your skull. Your friend dressed your scalp very well," the paramedic said, completing his examination.

"We found her semi-conscious. We've stabilized her and she's been on the sofa since we got back," she answered. "Does she need to be seen at a hospital?"

"Ma'am, the hospital has been destroyed and the nearest facility is four hours away," he answered. "We're still waiting for state and federal help and the emergency hospital is overwhelmed by the survivors. We've had ten tornado touchdowns confirmed. In my opinion, you should stay here."

Marie saw the fatigue and fear etched on the men's faces. She could only hope that they had time to evacuate their families before Hanna struck. She couldn't picture a more harrowing scenario than to save a stranger when your family is in peril.

"How destructive was Hanna?" David asked. "Are we better off staying put since we have the infrastructure, or should we go?"

"She took out half of the town and a great swath of the highway," the leader answered. "You seem to have survived the hurricane unscathed, and given your generators and your deep well, you are better off at home during this mayhem. Do you have enough supplies? Do you have food?"

"Yes, enough to last us for quite a while," Sophie answered, thanking the rescue team.

"We'll log our findings and your location and check back with you as soon as we have triaged the most pressing patients. Good luck!"

They watched the response crew leave on their raft, reassured by their visit and propelled into action by their near presence.

Turning to his friends, David said in calm voice, "I need to get to Marie's car. We need the supplies we left behind. I want to assess the neighborhood to see if we can sustain ourselves here. The highway will be impassable for days anyway."

"I'm coming with you," Marie answered, suffering no opposition. "Sophie is with Bunnie and Isabelle is drawing the tropicbirds." Her tone softened when she recognized his goodwill.

They prepped the canoe and filled two knapsacks with water and supplies and started canoeing towards Watson. Marie spotted more tropicbirds waving their long plumaged in the sea breeze. The Old Village had endured the storm and become a bird preserve.

"This place is unrecognizable," he said, pointing to a resin garden gnome's red hat embedded three inches deep in Mrs. Manigault's live oak.

"Oh my God!" said Marie, drawing his attention to a couple of vinyl records implanted into the old neighbor's wooden chicken coop siding.

They kept paddling on, anxious for downed power lines, careful of snakes. They reached Marie's street and saw the sandbags holding the water and standing guard. Isabelle's tree house was gone, along with the two large branches that supported it. The tree was leaning on the street, away from the house. The water had not breached her house and the wind had not splintered her shutters. She looked at her home in disbelief and gratitude. Her neighborhood had escaped a lot of the carnage.

"The water is receding a bit," Marie observed from her early canoe ride to Bunnie's home.

"You are right; the tide is ebbing."

"Should we evacuate or stay put?"

"I think we should stay put, shelter in place," he said. "The authorities will block access to the barrier islands and neighborhoods deemed inhabitable. We could be out of our homes for weeks or even months. There is a lot of wealth in this neighborhood. Homes in the Old Village, stores and any business left standing, will attract looters and unscrupulous contractors. Bunnie's house escaped the storm and would provide a great target."

"Looters?"

"Yes, martial law was enforced during Gabriella and we even had a dusk to dawn curfew. We had more than one hundred looters arrested after the storm. I say we take a page out of Bunnie's *Don't Tread on Me* book and stay."

"Are we in danger?" asked Marie, worried about her home and Bunnie's house. "And what is the *tread* reference about?"

"Looters are opportunistic and won't go after occupied homes. The National Guard will patrol the area and make sure we are fine. As for Bunnie's motto it dates to the American Revolution. The yellow flags you see around town with a timber rattlesnake below the words *Don't Tread on Me* and was the first American flag–and a symbol of our fight for independence. England used to send us convicted felons and Ben Franklin suggested we send them back our native rattlesnakes."

"He believed the rattlesnake represented the fighting spirit of the American people, lidless and forever watchful. The rattlesnake doesn't start a fight, but it doesn't back from one either," he continued. "It now represents American patriotism, support for civil movement, and even disagreement with the government."

"A fitting description for Bunnie," Marie said thinking about her gutsy friend.

Near Watson, Marie and David encountered more debris and devastation. Half of campus was destroyed but they still could identify Franklin and the new student center. They found the car where they had left it in the alley. Supplies, water, medications and food were left intact.

"Let's pack as many of the supplies as we can in the canoe and return back home. We need to get to the bottom of what happened to Bunnie. We won't be safe until we do."

They hurried back to the house relieved to see Bunnie resting and Isabelle playing with Dood. Sophie had set up the grill near the back porch and was grilling perishables from the fridge. They heard the generators humming in the background. David had plugged the freezer and fridge into one and the air conditioning and basic electricity in the other. The smell of the grilled burgers and vegetables was tantalizing and brought a sense of normalcy they didn't think they could experience again. They were ravenous for the comfort of good food. Sophie called everyone to the table and they rallied up around Bunnie who looked almost back to herself.

"I feel like a cat on a hot tin roof," she said. "I reckon I feel anxious about what I can't remember and worried about what I do remember. I see President Holzer looking into a large vault at objects and paintings. The tunnel was there, as I knew it would. I still don't understand why I went down there."

Marie, Sophie and David exchanged conspiratorial glances and smiles, knowing full well Bunnie could not resist the urge to snoop.

"I'm not certain I saw him behind me in the tunnel more than I felt his presence," she added, wrapping the blanket around her a little tighter.

"Don't worry about the fall," said Marie. "You uncovered a tunnel and an illegal collection. We will get to the bottom of the mystery."

"The Franklin Building survived the storm," Sophie said. "We'll have to go back to the safe when things settle."

"I plan to contact the Watson Board of Directors and the FBI's Art Crime Team," Marie insisted. "President Holzer will be held accountable for the federal crimes he committed. He was stealing history."

CHAPTER 28

THE LAST SUNFLOWER

Sophie reached Firenze Santa Maria Novella late in the afternoon. She disembarked the bullet train on time and proceeded to the exit of the busy station. Pulling her light carry-on suitcase, she trekked out of one of the largest train stations in Italy with ease. The place was bursting with travelers from every nation, their foreign voices echoing in the cavernous station, moving in all directions. Commuters dressed in trendy designer clothing side stepped masses of confused tourists. It reminded her of an old video game where agility, speed and accuracy led to success. Sophie avoided a family of four burdened by five heavy suitcases, guidebooks and maps, wheeling their belongings.

Walking briskly along Platform 16, she glanced at a statue and a plaque near the walkway and paused to read the inscription. They bore witness to the local families deported to Nazi concentration camps from that very station. Reminders of previous world wars abounded in Europe, cues of losses too great to forget. Most European hamlets had erected monuments or plaques commemorating lives lost, the need to remember and the need to forgive.

Sophie disliked the modern look of the train station, out of place in the midst of High Renaissance Florence. It was awkward and bullish, lacking in grace and beauty. The skylight of metal and glass seemed to hang in the air without the support of columns. The Mussolini's approved architectural rendition of modernism offended her. The building was a shock to her classical sensibility. The rawness of *pietra forta* lining the front of the building grated at her sense of style. It contrasted with the polished marble she often admired in churches, museums and palaces.

She reached inside her pocket for a worn letter and glanced at the familiar words. She memorized the address and waited at the curb for the next taxi cab. Fluent in Spanish, she could find similarities between the two Roman languages. Sophie hailed a cab and caught a ride to the heart of Florence.

Her plan was to stop at her hotel, freshen up and proceed on foot to her evening appointment with the lawyer. His letter, received a few weeks ago, had shattered her peace of mind. Seeking clarity, she had discussed it with her parents before booking the flight to Italy.

"Why now?" her mother asked during a late-night phone conversation.

"I need to see the whole picture."

"You've let go of so many people in your life recently," her mother replied. "You've focused on the transient and the ephemeral."

"I don't think biology is a fleeting thing," Sophie snapped, feeling inauthentic.

She knew full well who her real father had been for the past fifteen years. His goodwill, patience, love and commitment had forged the familial bonds of her childhood. Her stepfather had fulfilled all the roles a father should. He had protected her from the emotional ravages of abandonment. But he was not the object of her quest.

Sophie was strong enough to bear the impact of her father's desertion. She could hear the unspoken words of warning seep through her mother's words. If she let her weave her protective cocoon around her, it would immobilize her.

She had been careful, more cautious in fact than her mother could have predicted. She kept her knowledge of the hurricane events limited to Marie, David and Bunnie. The school has suppressed the real story. They had solved most of the riddle of the president's life; but she needed to tie a few loose ends–one of which burned a hole in her pocket. She fiddled with the creased letter, her fingers exploring its crumpled contours. What would this lawyer reveal she had not already imagined, dreaded or desired?

Her heart was aflutter with the beauty and the colors of Florence. Yet, her stomach lurched at the abrupt stops and turns of her taxi driver. His uncanny sense of depth helped him weave his mini Fiat through impossibly tight spots. He drove his car like a Roman charioteer at the games, with recklessness and abandon. After ten minutes of brazen commute, the car screeched to a halt in front of an imposing wooden studded door. Sophie stepped out on the pavement, the balmy air enveloping her and soothing her nerves.

An ancient metal knocker, welded to the door, prompted her to use the electric bell. A small window slid open and a sight of joyful wrinkles and sparkling eyes appeared. A pint-size woman opened the thick wooden door and led Sophie inside the courtyard. Her white hair twisted in a severe bun and her stark black dress contrasted with her boundless energy.

"*Buona sera*," the concierge welcomed her in a warm and honeyed voice. Sophie returned the greeting in Italian prompting a deluge of questions she could not answer.

The matron led Sophie to the lobby where a tall woman inspected a register at a marble counter. The hostess looked up and a mass of golden curls tumbled, framing her exquisite oval face and emerald eyes. Sophie was taken aback and tried not to stare. She had found in her hostess the live embodiment of Botticelli's vision of *Spring*. The tender brushes birthing perfection took flight before her. Sophie had walked into a living painting! Florence always triggered the most imaginative musings, she smiled.

Unaware of the artistic stirrings she caused in her guest, the young Italian woman led her visitor through a hallway painted with scenes of Florentine landscapes. Lush murals linked by a swirl of ivy danced along the tall arched ceiling. The hotel, a former palazzo and later convent, now catered to discerning travelers.

The hostess slid an antique iron key into the keyhole, opened the door, and ushered her guest into a serene island of plush comfort. The furniture was sparse but distinguished and the amenities simple but of the highest grade. The hotel, in a stroke of genius, had incorporated its past into an abode respecting both dualities–part convent and part palazzo. It illustrated that the faith and the crown could co-exist in harmony.

Sophie changed into a stylish auburn dress and tied her silky hair into a low chignon. She was eager to conclude her meeting with Signore De Luca and return to the haven of her hotel suite. His office was nearby, and she elected to walk. She stepped onto the street and felt the energy of the city enfold her.

Dozens of gleaming scooters, parked at meticulous angles, lined the narrow streets. They funneled a small stream of cars through the tortuous maze leading to Il Duomo. The polished stones absorbed the impact of her tired steps, lending comfort and ease to her walk.

Streets teemed with activity and the pent-up excitement released after a hot day spent out of the sun. The city woke up at night. Everywhere, people engaged in various forms of human activity. Commerce buzzed in and out of small shops selling first editions, paintings and antiques. Sophie glanced through an open window and saw artisans firing pottery in the back of a workshop. She recognized pots, plates and bowls, painted in the traditional style of the region. A cheese monger sold dozens of pungent cheeses from his shop, some with moldy rinds, others with distinctive golden colors. A corner shoe store offered sturdy leather sandals to a flock of nuns.

Among the teeming activity, large estates surrounded by tall imposing walls preserved the privacy of family life. Sophie wondered what manner of existence lay beyond these forbidding places. She turned the corner into a narrow street populated by small stalls. A slice of Il Duomo peeked through the optical window offered by the narrow street. The cathedral was massive and loomed large above her; as had the Treasury when stepping out of the *Siq*. Parts of the cathedral, restored to its younger days, gleamed in the evening light. Green, red and white marble, stripped of the grime of time, revealed exquisite patterns.

Sophie looked at the street to her right and found the *avvocato*'s corner office. The bronze street plaque professed generations of De Luca lawyers dating back to 1782. She rang and gained admittance to a set of steps scrambling up to the second floor. On top of the landing, Sophie met a tan man sporting the latest handmade *Ermenegildo Zegna* suit. He ushered her inside a well-appointed office lined with carved shelves, bursting with first edition treatises and legal tomes. Leather chairs, burnished with the patina of old age, had witnessed three centuries of clients buying legal services.

Umberto De Luca had a flair for the theatrical and the dramatic. He wore his business suits in an act as intimate as a beautiful woman donning her best lingerie. Little surgeries erased the telltale signs of natural aging and left him with a smooth, and out of place, baby face.

"My name is Signore De Luca," he said in a silky voice, taking and kissing Sophie's hand.

"Please call me Umberto. Your father and I were old friends," he said, finally releasing Sophie's hand. His hand grazing her back, he ushered her to a plush gilded chair by a balcony giving onto Il Duomo. He was uttering pleasantries to her distracted mind. Her gaze lingered on the magnificent dome. She could not imagine working in this office–she would be too distracted by the beauty surrounding her to get any work done.

"Let me first offer you my most sincere condolences. Such a loss, at such vital age!"

Sophie was at a loss for words. She had none to mourn someone she did not know. Her hands tucked away from the petulant Signore De Luca, she braced herself for his announcement.

"You have inherited a property in our beautiful Tuscan countryside," Umberto said. "The house sits on one hundred acres of land. I could take you there, if you wish."

It won't be necessary, thought Sophie, shuddering at more meetings with syrupy Signore De Luca. She told her parents she did not plan to accept the inheritance, but she was not sure anymore. She owed it to herself to visit the place and assess the house and grounds.

The president's wisdom and folly, magnified during the storm, defined his life and death. He had connected people and places and uncovered a secret long forgotten. In the end, the quest consumed him and cost him his life. Humanity would always be grateful to Charles Holzer for flushing out the artist's character and layering of his personality; but those who knew the president would condemn his extreme measures.

Sophie needed to understand the fascination this land exerted on Charles Holzer. She signed the paperwork Signore De Luca placed in front of her. He had none of the brisk and perfunctory business efficiency often displayed in America; instead he prolonged the meeting with an exaggerated sense of the dramatic. Each copy, when signed, was placed into an ornate binder at a creeping pace. Sophie was edgy and eager to leave.

Still wishing to strike common ground with his guest, and oblivious to her discomfort, Umberto tried a more personal approach. "You resemble him," he added with an intimate glance. This remark, more than his macho advances, sent Sophie hurrying to the refuge of her hotel room. She looked at Umberto, unable to respond to such an icebreaker. Sophie had come to Italy to break the link that anchored her to her father, not to reminisce about someone she didn't know. She took her leave with a binder containing rims of documents, some moderns and others quite ancient.

Back in her palatial convent, she picked up the paperwork and observed the owner's elegant and powerful signature. Perched on her bed, an Italian dictionary in one hand and her inheritance papers in the other, Sophie laughed. The cosmic joke had not escaped her dry sense of humor. The man she was trying to erase had made the task impossible. He had offered her a present too enticing to ignore.

She picked up the phone and dialed Signore De Luca's number to instruct him to place the house on the market, sight unseen. She wanted to flee back home and renounce the connection forever. Yet, the urge to complete her journey proved too tempting. She had to see *Villa Vittoria* for herself before letting go of the house and grounds. Her natural curiosity proved an obstacle too hard to overcome. She placed the phone back in its cradle and took a deep breath.

The next morning, Sophie stopped at the concierge's desk to make copies of her legal papers and pick up the keys to her rental car. The feeling of dread she had carried during her trip to Italy turned to excitement when she boarded her little Fiat.

She had come to Watson to learn about the president's character and proclivities. Her journey of discovery had uncovered an unsavory portrait of the man. She still cringed at the attack on Bunnie that could have taken her friend's life. Sophie wanted to close the chapter on President Holzer, but she knew that the puzzle would never be solved without a visit to his Tuscan property. She had braced herself for the nefarious depravity and Machiavellian deportment she was sure to find at the villa; but instead she had found peace, beauty and loveliness. The man she came to know through his sinister deeds and lies showed a surprising delicate side.

Sophie departed from Florence in the early morning hours. She drove through small villages more picturesque than the next. Along the way, country markets housed beneath large beam structures offered livestock, spices, fruits and vegetables to patrons. Rolling hills of maturing grapes, gorged with nectar, glistened under the bright sun. Rows of cypress trees punctuated her drive, connecting the dots, marking the way to her future. Sophie read signs promoting the award winning vineyards of the Val d' Orcia. She realized with pleasure that the *Brunello* originated from these grapes–one of her favorite wines. She reached her historic village dazzled by the beauty surrounding her.

Signore De Luca had shared with her some of the property's history. Sophie had inherited an estate tended by twenty generations of Rosa landowners and farmers. The line had survived for centuries to sadly thin, falter, wither and die. When the last heir died ten years ago, her father had purchased the house and restored the grounds to their original condition.

The approach to the estate veered among small farmhouses and an ancient church. She sensed the profound connections these people cultivated with their surroundings. The buildings enhanced, more than detracted, the beauty of the land. The deep green hues of spring had surrendered to the golden hues of fall and the land was gearing up for winter. Sophie stopped her car and stepped out onto the gravel path, mesmerized.

On the south side, a small olive grove flanked an imposing two-story stone villa. A walkway wove a stone path among lavender, rosemary and sage bushes, leading to a pool below. The scents of herbs drifted in the breeze. Potted red geraniums framed the terrace with a burst of color. Everywhere she looked, loveliness stared right back at her, welcoming her home. She was bewitched, and out of sorts. Yet, she felt an instantaneous rapport with a man who could enjoy such beauty.

Sophie was told the president had crafted provisions in his will for the care of his estate over several generations. The breadth and depth of his finances did not surprise her; she knew that he came from a political dynasty. What surprised her was his sense of the aesthetic and the authentic. Just as his collection showed, President Holzer was a lover of art and beauty. He had preserved his collection with love and care, and done the same for this estate. This was the place he had planned to retire to with his collection.

She was trespassing in a man's dream with only a thin blood kinship to recommend her. Sophie took a deep breath and crossed the threshold to a new reality. She walked into a home where the old and the new co-existed in elegance and harmony. Old tapestries of masters provided dramatic backgrounds for new pieces crafted by talented contemporary artists. Antique furniture and modern pieces ignored schools and eras and created their own narrative.

The house was a living canvas, each widow revealing distinctive paintings and playful hues. The outdoor light, diffused by shutters, dabbed the furniture with golden rays. Sophie climbed the steps to the second floor and walked into the master suite. A large four-poster bed, a writing desk, an imposing armoire and several chairs complemented the view. The wood smelled of lemon and beeswax. The left wing was ready to receive a large collection of paintings and sculptures. Blank walls with hanging hardware awaited a collection that would never come. The sculptures, now housed at Watson, would remain forever out of his reach. A sigh of relief escaped Sophie's lips when she realized no stolen paintings had entered Italy. With no international laws broken, the president's good name remained unsullied and her home was not a crime scene. She wanted to keep it that way.

She sat at the desk and retrieved the documents Signore De Luca had given her. Among the papers was a survey of several fields on her estate. She compared names and historical facts; she picked up her copy of the Florence files and read.

Several hours later, she had cross-referenced the genealogy of the owners of her estate with the names in the Florence files. This was the land where the master had experimented with aging marble. She was sure of it. President Holzer would have purchased no other house. She sat on the biggest discovery since his original breakthrough. He had intended to spend his retirement excavating his land and searching for additional treasures. She shuddered to think what laid in the rich Tuscan earth that now belonged to her. Her first reaction was to call her friends at Watson and share her thoughts with them. She picked up the phone, dialed the numbers and stopped to place the headphone back in the cradle. She stepped out on the balcony and looked at the night sky with wonder.

There it laid before her, in spidery cursive black letters, and she understood the connection. Michelangelo's surrogate mother, his beloved wet nurse, had numerous relatives near Settignano and the young artist found in their homes and hearth the warmth he never experienced in his father's house. Marble touched his heart unlike any other medium. It lived in his blood and sinews, his muscles and his aching back.

In the library, Sophie discovered a treasure trove of books, folios and drawings, all pertaining to Michelangelo. It appeared that everything ever written about him was in this house. Books in French, Italian, Spanish and English covered every surface, desk, tables and even chairs. They contained beautiful illustrations, delicate drawings and exquisite anatomical sketches. She also found books on archeological excavations and tools.

She fell asleep on the master bed, jetlagged and confused, and woke up at midday hungry and disoriented. The immediate connection she felt with the property and the natural beauty of the place kept clashing with her knowledge of its former owner. To clear her head, she picked up the picnic wicker basket prepared by the hotel and walked the grounds, looking for the best place to sit down for lunch.

In the shade an olive grove dotted with wild legumes and late blooming wild flowers, Sophie found an old stone studio with walls covered in yellow and grey lichen. She looked at the metal ring Signore De Luca had given her, and tried a few iron keys before settling on the right one. Opening the studio, she found an empty room with shelves lining the walls up to the ceiling and ancient garden tools stacked in a corner. Ancient stone dust covered every nook and cranny, windows and tables. She ran a finger along the shapes of missing statues and busts once stored on the shelves. She closed the door and locked it with reverence having peeked at a mystery. Outside the studio, a meadow of late blooming sunflowers made a stand among their dried, head-bowing and brown counterparts. The bright flowers reminded her of Bunnie's resilience, tenacity and grit. Sophie thought of the Carolinas and her friends awaiting her return. They were preparing for the grand reopening of Watson half a world away. She planned to be back on time for the occasion.

Sophie sat on the stone bench facing the sunflower field, her back to the studio. Basking in the late afternoon sun, she opened her basket, grabbed a sandwich bursting with fresh slices of mozzarella, ripe tomatoes, basil and prosciutto and began eating to the songs of cicadas. She sipped on a glass of *Rosso di Montalcino* and looked at the excavating documents she brought from the main house. The grid aligned itself with the topography of the property. A detailed area showcased the place she was standing on. The documents illustrated the beginning of a methodical search.

How could he keep this excavation a secret? Locals elevated gossip to an art form in these little villages; and his activities, requiring labor, would be noticed. *He planned to keep it all to himself,* she realized. Just as he had stolen the Michelangelo sculptures and the paintings; he had no intention of making the discovery of additional sculptures public. She thought of the hubris of such a quest. Was he one of those ancient pharaohs who took their tomb builders along with them in their journey to the afterlife? She was sitting on a time tomb she did not know how to diffuse.

She thought of her friends, ignoring the real purpose of her travel plans and awaiting her return. Where could she begin her tale without seeming totally disingenuous? How could she explain the pull that this place exerted on her heart? Sophie could no more accept the connection than she could deny it. This left her frustrated, sad and apprehensive. She had to unburden herself to her friends and seek their forgiveness and guidance.

Her picnic completed, she looked inside the studio and saw the old tools standing in the corner. She picked up a rusted shovel with a sturdy wood handle and walked among the sunflowers, looking for the brightest late bloomer in a sea of dead blossoms. The sun shone brightly on its petals. She smiled at the flower, set her shovel on the ground and began to dig.

CHAPTER 29
GOWNS AND TAMS

One year to the date of Hanna's passage, Marie stood on the steps of the Franklin Building going over the last minute preparations for the ribbon cutting of the grand opening of the Charles Holzer Renaissance Wing. The Michelangelo sculptures were displayed prominently in the center of the gallery, awaiting the latest rounds of authentication. She had invited prominent Italian art historians and was pleased to note all had accepted. Bunnie had been very helpful in organizing the event. High Renaissance experts were coming from across the world. Sophie had just returned from a trip abroad, making contacts with colleagues overseas and inviting them to the ceremony.

Marie decided to merge the reopening of Franklin with the addition of the Charles Holzer Wing. It provided her the occasion to invite members of the public and the media to two major but separate events: the opening of the new wing and the introduction of the Michelangelo sculptures. *The wheels of academia spin very slowly across the pond,* she thought. The controversy was sure to rage for years, if not decades.

Their lives had changed drastically since the morning they walked out of the campus scarred, exhausted and disbelieving their eyes. David was right, and they had since associated the aftermath of the storm with the old beaten up washing machine, sensing that a monumental cleanup had just begun. *Amazing what a little comic relief can do,* she smiled.

Marie had stayed at Watson determined to study and curate President Holzer's collection. Her daughter, undaunted by the passage of the hurricane, recognized she was part an effort greater than her little self. She loved staying at Ms. Bunnie's, playing with her new puppy and collecting eggs and feeding the goat Rosalie.

Bunnie's house had weathered the storm like a true grit southerner. The force of the storm had peeled off layers of paint from the old pile. The house looked like a bleached canvas awaiting a bright nautical hue. The hurricane shutters had worked their magic and kept the destructive gusts of wind from penetrating the house and destroying generations of memories. Bunnie and her friends had worked incessantly on the house for a year and the renovations brought forth a home rejuvenated and proud again.

Marie's new position as Dean of the Fine Arts Department kept her busy. Once President Holzer's illegal collection was brought to the attention of the Board, a new narrative began to emerge. Marie wasn't completely comfortable with it, but she understood the need to keep the discovery free of modern scandal, if it became part of the public record. *This part of history belongs to the ages,* she thought. In the end, President Holzer was recognized as the agent of discover; the school was envied its good luck; and Marie was hired to curate the discovery. The tale course-corrected and gave the collection back to its legal owner. *A pretty convenient ending,* she admitted.

She looked at the stanchions gleaming in the sun, the wide red ribbon and matching bows gently blowing in the sea breeze, the red carpet awaiting the arrival of the dignitaries. David performed a last sound check. Sophie directed a group of undergraduates to their posts, programs in hand. The school's chamber orchestra practiced its overture. Marie had organized a program laced with High Renaissance references mixed with modern southern subtleties. She hoped to greet her guests with the tradition they deserved and the innovation they sought. She had grown to love the South with its beautiful vistas, painful past, genteel facade and vibrant future. It resembled the artist and the age they were celebrating. She wanted to build a bridge to connect both experiences and honor all present.

David looked at Marie from the stage. He had grown to depend on their friendship as he would a cold glass of water after a day laboring under the Carolina sun. Growing his business, renovating Bunnie's home, and taking care of his small circle of friends had given a new direction and purpose to his life. The acute loneliness he felt over the past ten years was dissipating, replaced by friendly faces.

David and Marie had been too busy over the past year to embark in a romantic relationship. Instead, they developed a deep friendship based on their common interests and their similar sense of humor. Marie had shared her painful past with him and he sometime felt acutely her husband's presence near her. He waited for her to cast off the shadows and let go of the pain. He had initially thought that she would return to Pennsylvania in the aftermath of the storm; but she had welcomed her new life with vigor and determination. He watched her grow in grace and peace and could not imagine his life without her smile, gentleness, intelligence and beauty. They had reached a good place and he planned to ask her on an official date after the opening ceremonies.

Distracted by thoughts of him, Marie looked at David in the sound booth and waved at him from across the stage. He was getting ready to propose a date for next weekend and had even discussed the location details with Bunnie and babysitting duties with Sophie. He was ready; Bunnie had told her in confidence. Marie's interest in David had grown from a very strong friendship to much more. She was eager to experience their first kiss and lay in his arms. After months of very hard work, he would be her prize, her recompense for her renewed strength and courage in the midst of chaos. She would be his tender acknowledgement that he was not alone in the world anymore.

The aftermath of the storm had been mind-numbing for most of the community. Emergency helicopters circled the town daily, scattering Bunnie's fowls and scaring her cats. For months, the rumble of chainsaws went on from dawn until dusk, grating at everyone's sanity. The cleanup task was almost too much to bear, even for Bunnie who had lost significantly less than her neighbors. The pile of debris at the municipal dump never seemed to go down despite continuous hauling by public workers. The thirty-foot high heap refused to budge and kept on growing.

The entire state had received emergency funding and Bunnie had repaired her home with the federal help she received. Unscrupulous contractors had descended on the region like a swarm of locusts, exploiting vulnerable homeowners. David proved invaluable in protecting Bunnie's home and her interests. He accompanied her to the FEMA's office and helped fill out all the forms and supervise contractors. They worked from the inside out, bringing the plumbing and electricity up to code, and gutting the upstairs bedrooms. Ten months after Hanna, Bunnie's home had a new roof and a shining coat of paint.

New homes, twice the size of the previous abodes, cropped up on the barrier islands. The beach designs had replaced the small brick ranch homes. Like a rejuvenating fire burning a forest to ashes, Hanna's destruction erected gleaming new multi-million dollar homes.

"I've heard that some owners, instead of boarding their homes left them unprotected, inviting complete destruction," said Bunnie. "I know someone who left the door of his home open before Hanna's landfall."

"Don't let this get out or your friend could be liable for insurance fraud," warned Marie.

Her friend had recovered her spunk and home rule spirit. Just as new rows of identical beach homes cropped up along the coast, Bunnie's Victorian home survived and maintained its distinction. Repaired to her old glory, Bunnie's house shone with strength and authenticity.

"The fundraiser for the Henderson Lighthouse is scheduled for next week," Bunnie said, a master at redirecting. "I have tickets for all of us."

"We wouldn't miss it. I will finally get to visit the place where so many blue crabs met their untimely deaths at your hands," Marie laughed. "You could teach Isabelle the art of crabbing."

Bunnie recalled the ivory handle knife in her bedroom's drawer chest and added, "I have all the equipment she needs. We'll go next week. Remind me to get some chicken necks."

Marie's ear piece crackled, announcing the arrival of the dignitaries. She smiled as the new president, senior officials, heads of departments and academia in full regalia proceeded down the aisle to their respective seating. The pomp and circumstance of such events never ceased to amaze her. She loved the rich fabrics of caps and gowns, the mantle of academic finery at its finest. She had donned on her own calf-length robe and tasseled tam, a remnant of European pageantry and drafty halls. David had helped her adjust her hood, honor cords, medal and tassel.

"I'm so proud of everything you've accomplished," he had said, watching her get ready in her office. She was a sight to behold. He loved her keen wit and infectious chuckles. She seemed to laugh much more now. He found her intelligence one of her sexiest qualities and the medieval outfit she wore only emphasized it. *She looked so darn hot!* He wanted to take her in his arms and shower her with kisses. Her scent and warmth wove tendrils of longing in his body, but he knew the day was fast approaching when he'd be hers. "Spin around young lady," he said turning her around to make sure everything was in place.

The Star-Spangled Banner performed by the Watson University Brass Ensemble resonated on the Great Lawn, enveloping visitors and dignitaries in a patriotic mood.

Marie heard Emily Gaillard, the first female president of Watson, extol the virtues of President Holzer. Her predecessor had governed the school with a fair and progressive hand, she said. She listed the numerous awards and distinctions he acquired during his twenty-year tenure. She was building interest and credentials for the man before unveiling his final contribution to the school. President Charles Holzer's extraordinary knowledge of the High Renaissance era allowed him to connect Michelangelo's early sculptures to several pieces the school purchased at a country auction, near Settignano.

The new president avoided all controversy by declaring the authentication process still ongoing. She skirted the issue of forgery like a pro and focused on the artist and the discovery. At the heart of the matter was the authentication of documents linking Buonarroti to the purchase of several blocks in the Settignano region, one which probably was used to sculpt the Sleeping Cupid and other pieces preceding the David and the Pieta. In question was establishing the custody record. What this discovery implied had already ignited furor in the art world and would have to be addressed by the combined talents of President Gaillard and Doctor Caldwell.

The Watson Board of Directors went on full damage control mode after the passage of Hanna. Marie reported Bunnie's attack in the tunnel and the presence of the safe in the Franklin Building. Upon investigating the content of the vault and assessing the extent of the theft, the Board assigned her the direction of the Fine Arts Department. They urged her to consider the best interests of the school, and the impact that a scandal would have on the Michelangelo discovery. She was asked to right a wrong committed by President Holzer.

Marie had accepted, conscious that lines were blurred, but intent on making sure the art regained its rightful place in the museum. Chief Glenburn was dismissed following mysterious legal troubles. The Board squashed the story and it never made it to the newspapers, busy with post Hanna stories. Looking at the majesty surrounding the opening of the new wing, Marie knew that the outcome was far from transparent, but it was practical–given the circumstances.

CHAPTER 30
EPILOGUE

"I'll meet you at the reception," Sophie told Marie, taking her leave after the ribbon cutting. She drove to the florist and purchased a single sunflower. She returned home and picked up a bag from her overseas travel. The flower in one hand and the bag in the other, she walked the couple of blocks to the Old Village historic cemetery where some of the past presidents of Watson were buried. She showed the cemetery guard her credentials and gained access to the school crypt.

Most presidents were interred in their personal family plots, but few elected to rest on school grounds. In President Holzer's case, the school had claimed him. He was a hero; forever associated with the fame he had won the school. The Michelangelo sculptures were going to generate interest for generations to come and rewrite conventional art history. Charles Holzer would be forever associated with this discovery and earn a place of distinction in academia.

Sophie reflected on the reversal of fortune inflicted upon a man with superior belief in his abilities. She sat next to his coffin and placed the sunflower in a marble vase. Thoughts of Tuscany came back unbidden, bringing flashes of sadness for a life cut short in such a dramatic way–so far from the place he yearned for. President Holzer had lost everything when victory seemed assured. His body was recovered on the top of a live oak tree ten miles from campus, mangled and in shocking condition. A positive ID was made with his wallet containing his credentials. A gun registered in his name was found in his pocket. He had wandered in the eye of the storm when a tornado plucked him away, sucking the life from him.

She did not want to think about the gun and the ramifications that such a presence meant. She had reached a quota for the evil her father could inflict upon the world. The attempted murder of innocent people was not comprehensible to her. She wanted to keep an area unblemished where only beauty would reside. That place was tangible, she had witnessed it. President Holzer was able to recognize beauty and experience rapture. She had seen the art he collected and the Italian estate he had renovated. A measure of good must still have resided inside him to drive him to protect such beauty.

Sophie's tears came upon her in a torrent of mute regrets. The raging flow of grief shook her to the core–the type of tears and distress that seize the brain and the heart in agony. She cried herself into a state of despondency for what could never be: a connection she would not recognize and a father she would to keep hidden.

She rose, prepared to leave, and reached into her bag for a piece of antique marble. *The hand of God carved from the inside.* She reverently placed the sculpture on her father's tomb. It shone, eclipsing the darkness of the crypt. The patina of the piece echoed the spirit of ancient sculptors. The index finger fully stretched, radiating divine energy, discharged the spark of life.

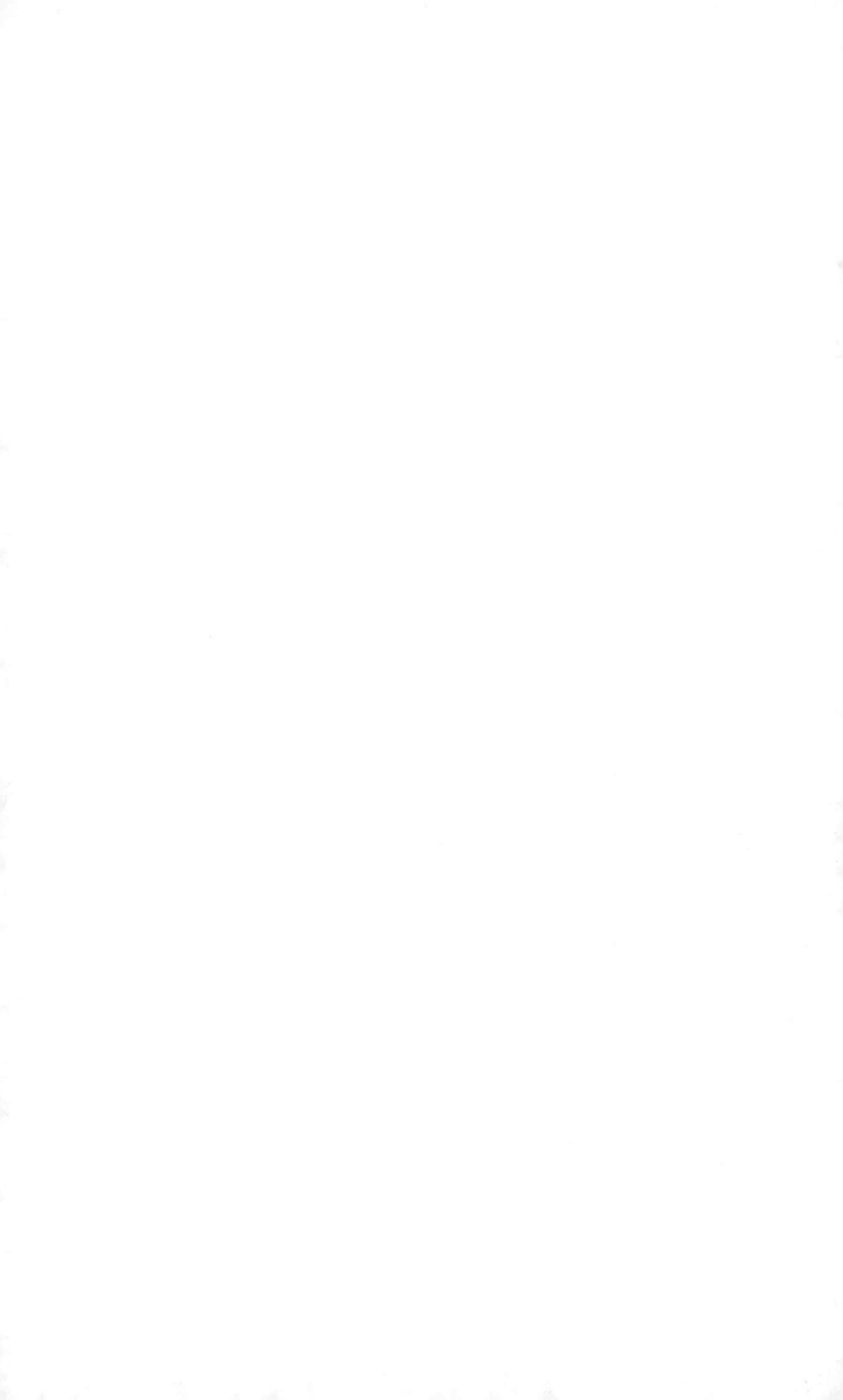

www.ingramcontent.com/pod-product-compliance
Lightning Source LLC
LaVergne TN
LVHW010648110826
845149LV00014B/2991

* 9 7 8 0 9 9 8 2 6 2 8 0 2 *